CHAPTER ONE

It began when Geoff disappeared.

The last words he said were, 'Where do you want to go then?' And Tom was about to reply that he couldn't really think of anywhere worth going when, without warning, with barely even a sound, the entire wedge of earth and grass on which Geoff had been sitting came away from the side of the hill and slid with astonishing speed down the side of the quarry in front of them.

Tom watched in astonishment. Geoff had his rucksack on his lap, a can of drink poised in one hand, and there was scarcely time for the look of surprise to register on his face before the earth hit the bottom of the quarry. There was a rumble like passing thunder . . .

And he disappeared.

Tom looked at the place where Geoff had been sitting, then at the path that had been scythed through the undergrowth on the side of the slope, and finally at the dark hole at the bottom of the hollow into which his friend had vanished.

The whole thing had taken a little less than three seconds.

'Geoff?' he called, and the sound of his voice echoed round the countryside. 'Geoff, are you all right?'

There was no reply.

Tom hesitated. It was one of those times when fast, decisive action was required, but he had never been good at rapid decisions. He was the sort of boy who needs time to think. Quite a lot of time usually, and for anything of real importance, he preferred several days' notice.

He could go back and get help, but he knew that would take time, and Geoff might need him now. Alternatively, he could climb down and see what had happened, but if Geoff really *was* hurt, what could he actually do?

Decisions . . .

'Geoff!' he called again. 'Can you hear me?'

'Aaaaaagh!' A sudden wail came up from the ground. Distorted, muffled, but not encouraging.

'Geoff? What is it?'

'Aaaaaaaaaaagh!' The cry was followed this time by an odd scrabbling sound.

Tom threw off his rucksack, rolled over on to his stomach and lowered himself over the edge of the quarry. As his feet searched for a foothold, his

PUFFIN BOOKS

Aquila

Andrew Norriss was born in Scotland in 1947, went to university in Ireland and taught history in a sixth-form college in England for ten years before becoming a full-time writer. In the course of twenty years, he has written and co-written some hundred and fifty episodes of situation comedies and children's drama for television, and has written four books for children, including *Aquila*, which won the Whitbread Children's Book of the Year in 1997.

He lives very contentedly with his wife and two children in a village in Hampshire, where he acts in the local dramatic society (average age sixty-two), sings in the church choir (average age seventy-two) and for real excitement travels to the cinema in Basingstoke.

Books by Andrew Norriss

AQUILA
BERNARD'S WATCH
MATT'S MILLION
THE TOUCHSTONE

ANDREW NORRISS

AQUILA

PUFFIN

For my wife, Jane,
who has always been a biggish sort of eagle

PUFFIN BOOKS

Published by the Penguin Group
Penguin Books Ltd, 80 Strand, London WC2R 0RL, England
Penguin Group (USA), Inc., 375 Hudson Street, New York, New York 10014, USA
Penguin Books Australia Ltd, 250 Camberwell Road, Camberwell, Victoria 3124, Australia
Penguin Books Canada Ltd, 10 Alcorn Avenue, Toronto, Ontario, Canada M4V 3B2
Penguin Books India (P) Ltd, 11 Community Centre, Panchsheel Park, New Delhi – 110 017, India
Penguin Group (NZ), cnr Airborne and Rosedale Roads, Albany, Auckland 1310, New Zealand
Penguin Books (South Africa) (Pty) Ltd, 24 Sturdee Avenue, Rosebank 2196, South Africa

Penguin Books Ltd, Registered Offices: 80 Strand, London WC2R 0RL, England

www.penguin.com

First published 1997
This edition published 2001

19

Copyright © Andrew Norriss, 1997
All rights reserved

The moral right of the author has been asserted

Set in Plantin

Made and printed in England by Clays Ltd, St Ives plc

British Library Cataloguing in Publication Data
A CIP catalogue record for this book is available from the British Library

ISBN-13: 978-0-14-130895-1

www.greenpenguin.co.uk

MIX
Paper from
responsible sources
FSC
www.fsc.org   FSC™ C018179

Penguin Books is committed to a sustainable
future for our business, our readers and our
planet. This book is made from paper certified
by the Forest Stewardship Council.

fingers gripped the grass – but the earth beneath them instantly gave way, and he started to slide.

Halfway down he grabbed a branch to try to slow his rate of descent, but the tree was dead, the wood broke off in his hand and a moment later he was turning, sliding, tumbling and falling all the way to the bottom before disappearing into the darkness.

Winded and blinded, he struggled to his feet. Slowly, his eyes adjusted to the light.

He was in a cave. The only sound was of water dripping softly from the roof above, and the rock beneath his feet felt damp and cold. Over to one side he could just make out his friend sitting on the ground nursing an elbow.

'Are you all right?'

Geoff nodded.

Tom looked at him carefully.

'You're sure?'

'Fine.' Geoff was recovering his breath. 'Absolutely fine.'

'Really?'

'Yeah.' Geoff nodded a little more certainly. 'Really. Fine.'

Tom's shoulders relaxed a little, but his grip on the piece of branch he was still holding did not loosen.

'So . . . why the screaming?'

'Sorry about that.' Geoff smiled a little sheepishly. 'I suppose it was seeing him over there.'

Tom turned round to where Geoff was pointing.

'Aaaaaaaaaaaaaaagh!' he screamed.

'Missing?' The Deputy Headmistress had the sort of penetrating voice that can only be developed from years of shouting across playgrounds and playing fields. 'Who's missing?'

Mr Urquart winced. 'It's two of the Year Sevens. They were supposed to be back at twelve thirty but . . . but they're not here.'

Mr Urquart was understandably worried. This was the first school trip he had organized, and the Peak District National Park had seemed the ideal place for so many learning experiences. He had not banked on losing two of the children before they had even sat down to have lunch.

Miss Taylor looked at her watch. It was twelve thirty-five.

'Boys or girls?'

'Boys.' Mr Urquart hurriedly consulted a list on his clipboard. 'Geoffrey Reynolds and Thomas Baxter.'

'Ah!' Miss Taylor relaxed, took a can of ginger beer from her briefcase and pulled the ring. 'You hadn't given them any written work by any chance, had you?'

'Well, they had a worksheet.' Mr Urquart produced the master copy from his file. 'I gave one of these to all their form, but I did emphasize they *must* be back before lunch so that –'

Miss Taylor sat down at one of the picnic tables with her drink.

'I shouldn't worry about it. Here.' She offered her colleague a sandwich. 'Have something to eat.'

'But the boys –'

'The boys'll be fine.' She gave him an encouraging smile. 'I'll bet anything you like they're sitting somewhere quietly at the moment, doing nothing at all.'

'You're sure?'

'Believe me. I know those two.'

Tom and Geoff sat quietly on the ground, doing nothing.

'It's all right,' said Geoff. 'He's dead. I didn't realize it at first, but he's definitely dead.'

'Yes.' Tom nodded. 'I can see that.'

He was not an authority on dead bodies, but he knew that not having any skin – or anything else except bones, really – was not a sign of peak health.

And anyway, there was the armour. You see a skeleton wearing a suit of armour, clutching a sword in the bones of one hand and a shield in the other, and you know it's dead. It has to be dead.

Tom just wished it wouldn't keep looking at him like that.

'I'd say he was Roman.' Geoff got up for a closer look. 'I've got a model dressed like that at home.'

'We need to try and get out.' Tom stood up and looked at the hole in the roof through which they had fallen. It was their only way out of the cave, but it was too high to reach. 'Any ideas?'

Geoff did not reply. He had taken the sword from the skeleton, scattering finger-bones all over the ground, and was experimentally stabbing with it at the air.

'I suppose if we piled some of these rocks into the middle, we might be able to stand on them,' said Tom. 'Or maybe I could climb on to your shoulders and then . . . Geoff, are you listening?'

'Sorry.' Geoff had stopped waving the sword around, and was staring into the cave. 'I was just wondering what that was.'

'It's a skeleton.'

'No, no, I meant that thing. Over there.' Geoff pointed in a direction slightly to one side and behind the dead body.

Tom peered nervously into the darkness.

'It's just a rock. They're all rocks, you can . . .'

He stopped. The rock Geoff was pointing to was a different colour to those around it, and had a curiously regular shape. As they walked towards it, they could see that, whatever it was, it certainly wasn't a rock.

It was large, smooth, a dull red in colour and shaped rather like a small boat. The front was pointed in a smooth upward curve that reminded Tom of the nose of a dolphin.

'It's got writing on it.' He leaned forward to brush away the dust with his sleeve. On the upper surface,

someone had painted a series of letters in go[...]
before he could make out what they were, Geoff
called him.

'Tom?'

There were two seats let into the centre of whatever it was, and Geoff was sitting in one of them. He
was beckoning to Tom, and staring intently in front
of him.

'What?'

Geoff pointed and Tom came round to look. On
the surface in front of the seats, a green light glowed
in the dark.

'What did you do?'

'I didn't do anything. It just came on.'

'It came on?'

'I just sat down and it came on.' Geoff pointed.
'Like that one.'

A small orange light had appeared beside the
green one. A moment later it was joined by another.

And another.

Silently, Tom climbed in to sit beside Geoff. They
watched as the lights continued to flick on until they
extended to cover the whole board in front of them
and then spread along the panel that stretched
between them to the floor.

At the same time, the boys became aware of a
faint humming, an almost inaudible vibration that
they felt rather than heard, culminating in a ping that
reminded Tom of a microwave oven telling you the
pizza was ready.

as that.

.' Geoff reached out a hand. Directly in
of him were two horizontal handles and
between them a circle of four large, blue lights
arranged like the petals of a flower. 'I wonder what it
is?'

'What?'

'This. What do you think it is?'

'It's . . .' Tom shrugged. 'Well, it's a machine.'

'Yes, but what's it for?' Geoff ran a finger
cautiously over the surface of one of the lights. 'I
wonder if we could find out.'

'What are you doing?'

'They're not just lights, are they?' Leaning forward, Geoff stared intently at the surface under his
hand. 'They're buttons, you see? I reckon if you
pushed one of these –'

'You can't do that!' Tom stared in horror at his
friend. 'You don't know what'll happen!'

Geoff said nothing. Obviously they didn't know
what would happen. It was why he wanted to push a
button and find out. His finger still hovered over the
group of blue lights.

'At least let's think about it first,' Tom pleaded.

'Think about it?'

'Just for a minute or two. It might help.'

Reluctantly, Geoff sat back and thought about it.
But the more he thought, the more it struck him that
you could think for ever and still not know anything.
There was only one way to really *know*.

'I'll try this one.' He reached out and stabbed one of the blue lights firmly with a forefinger.

Tom opened his mouth to protest but before he could speak, the world disappeared in an explosion of light and noise accompanied by a thin, high-pitched wailing sound, which Tom only slowly real-ized was his own voice.

'Frightened?' said Mr Urquart. 'You think they're frightened?'

'Terrified.' Miss Taylor brushed the crumbs off her skirt. 'Both of them. It's a straight biological reaction. You mention the possibility of written work and their feet feel this irresistible urge to move in the opposite direction.'

'I see.'

'It's a form of allergy, really. You know I've actu-ally seen Tom come out in a rash when someone asked him to write a poem?'

'I'd no idea . . .'

'I should have warned you. It doesn't matter so much in the classroom, of course, but out here . . . well, they just run away.'

'I see . . .'

Miss Taylor paused for a moment to tell a child half a mile away to stop picking its nose. 'What have you got planned for their group this afternoon?'

Mr Urquart picked up his file. 'At one thirty, I was taking them up to see the Hall . . .'

'That's when they'll turn up. One thirty.' Miss

Taylor took a bite out of her third pork pie. 'They'll have some story about losing the worksheet in a gale, chasing after it, getting lost. Little blighters.' She patted Mr Urquart on the knee. 'The important thing is not to spoil your lunch bothering about it.'

When Tom stopped screaming, he realized the main reason it was still dark was that he had his eyes closed. He opened them to find everything was white. White light, white mist, white everything.

Geoff was still sitting beside him. He had gone a bit white as well.

'Are we still alive?'

'I think so.' Geoff forced a smile. 'I'm still breathing and things.'

'Where are we?'

'Ah . . .' Geoff hesitated. 'Well, I had a look and we're still sort of in the same place, but . . . up a bit.'

'Up a bit?'

Geoff nodded. 'If you look over the side . . .'

Tom looked over the side and immediately wished he hadn't. The ground was still there, but a very long way away. Between the clouds, he could see the vast pattern of fields, trees, a river winding through the valley . . . He hurriedly closed his eyes again.

'I reckon it's about half a mile.' Geoff sounded calm, though his voice was pitched a little higher than normal. 'But it's OK, I know what to do.' He reached forward. 'If that one made us go up, then this one –' he pointed to the button underneath it –

'should make us go down.'

'Don't touch anything!' Tom gripped Geoff's arm.

'What?'

'Don't touch it. Leave it alone, just don't . . . touch anything!'

'We don't have any choice, Tom!' Geoff spoke quietly. 'Unless you want to stay up here for ever.'

'I know, but . . .' Tom was still holding Geoff's arm. 'I think we should sit here and think about it first, all right? Let's . . . think about it.'

They sat together in silence for several minutes while Tom thought about it.

There was, he eventually decided, only one thing to do if they were ever going to get down.

'OK,' he said. 'Try it. But slowly, OK? Very slowly.'

Geoff reached out and gently pushed the button.

Several seconds passed.

'Is anything happening?'

'Yes,' said Tom. 'We're going backwards.'

CHAPTER TWO

It was very simple once you knew. There were four of the blue lights. Two of them made you go up or down, the other two sent you forwards or backwards. The harder you pushed, the faster you went.

There was one heart-stopping moment when Geoff grasped the handle in front of him, and the whole machine swung over on to its side. The boys hung there for a second, and were just starting to topple out, when Geoff instinctively reached out to clutch the other handle and, as he did so, the machine righted itself.

The handles either side of the blue lights responded to pressure. You pushed them as if you were trying to steer a motorbike, and as you did so, the whole machine swung round. Pull them up, and you pointed upwards. Push them down or to the side, and that's where the nose went.

The whole thing, Geoff thought, required slightly less skill than riding a tricycle. You gripped the handles, used your thumbs to push the buttons, and off you went.

'A child could do this,' he said cheerfully, as he swung them down and to the left in a banking curve that would take them through a gap in the clouds.

'You think you can get us down?' asked Tom.

'No problem.' Through the cloud, Geoff turned in a gentle spiral to the right. 'That's what I've been saying. Anyone could do this, you –'

'If you can get us down,' said Tom, 'I think you should do it. I think you should do it now.'

'OK . . .' Geoff pushed forward, the nose dipped, and a slightly increased pressure from his left thumb sent them sinking towards the earth.

As they got closer, he swung briefly to the left to avoid a clump of trees, and they finally came to rest on the edge of a cornfield. He swung round a few times, lifted his hands from the controls, and looked down at the flattened circle of corn beneath them.

'That should give the farmer something to think about.' He turned to Tom. 'How are you feeling?'

Tom was already scrambling out of his seat. He had never quite realized before what a wonderful thing it was to stand, simply to stand, on firm ground. It would be even better when his knees had stopped shaking.

Geoff climbed out to stand beside him. It was his

first chance to get a proper look at the machine that had catapulted them so extraordinarily into the air, and the first thing he noticed was that it wasn't actually on the ground, but hovering motionless a few inches above the flattened corn.

It hadn't moved so much as a millimetre as he and Tom had climbed out. Not even a tremor. And although it hung in mid-air, it somehow gave the impression of being more solidly positioned there than the ground beneath it.

The letters Tom had noticed painted on the front were now clearly visible. The gold was faded and peeling but still legible.

'What does it say?'

Tom came round to look. 'Aquila,' he read.

Aquila. It was a good name, Geoff decided. 'You think it's Roman?'

'What?'

'The man in the cave was Roman. I suppose this must be as well.'

'I don't see how it could be.' Tom frowned. 'Romans didn't have flying machines, did they?'

Geoff tried to remember. They had done the Romans with Miss Spatchull in Year Six. He didn't recall her saying anything about flying, but it might have been a lesson he had missed.

'You think it's newer than that?' He gazed doubt-fully at the machine. 'It doesn't look new. It looks more sort of . . . old. Very old.'

Without knowing why, Tom had to agree. He

stepped forward to finger a dent at the back where a large corner of one metal fin was twisted and discoloured.

'Did we do that?'

Geoff shook his head. 'It was like that when we got it. Come on.' He swung a foot on to the side wing of Aquila and pulled himself up and back into the seat. 'I vote we tell Mr Urquart it all started when his worksheet blew away in a gale. And we'll say we were chasing it, when . . . What's the matter?'

Tom stared at him. 'What are you doing?'

'We have to get back.' Geoff settled in his seat. 'We've missed lunch already.'

'You're going to *fly* there?'

'Why not?' Geoff grinned. 'Oh, boy! Their faces when they see this . . .'

Tom hesitated.

'Come on!' said Geoff. 'It'll be fun.'

'Yeah . . .' Tom stepped slowly up to Aquila. 'Fun.'

'Right,' said Miss Taylor. 'Where exactly were they supposed to go?'

Mr Urquart pointed to the map attached to his master worksheet. 'Along here. The route marked in green. It was an exercise in map-reading, you see, and they had to –'

'If you sent them that way, they've probably gone over here.' Miss Taylor pointed in the opposite direction. 'What's all this?'

'That's a quarry.'

'Quarry?'

'And some old lead mines.' Mr Urquart swallowed nervously. 'And caves. There's a lot of caves round here. It's what makes it such an interesting area, geographically . . .'

'Perfect.' Grimly, Miss Taylor stood up and turned to face the children. 'Listen up, everybody. Pay attention, please!'

All heads turned in her direction, including a party of old-age pensioners on the far side of the picnic area, who guiltily put down their cups of tea and stopped talking.

'You probably all know by now that we've got two people missing,' said Miss Taylor. 'I am going off to find them and bring them back. I just want to make it clear that if anyone else is foolish enough to get lost this afternoon, they will be travelling back to school with their feet tied to the back axle of the coach. Understood? All right, carry on.'

'You don't think they've had an accident, do you?' asked Mr Urquart.

Miss Taylor picked up her map. 'They will have when I get to them,' she muttered, and strode off, stony-faced, into the trees.

The flight back to the quarry was not as bad as Tom had expected. They travelled at a few metres above the ground, which was a lot less frightening than being several thousand metres in the air, and he had to concede it was the most extraordinary sensation.

It was like being a bird, but without all the bother of remembering to flap your wings. Aquila sailed over the ground with less effort than it took to push a telephone button, and in total silence.

A couple of cows gazed indifferently up at them as they crossed one field, and a flock of sheep ran away from their shadow in the next. They waved at a couple of cyclists when they flew over a road, and laughed as one of them fell off his bike in surprise.

And when, finally, they swept over the top of the hill behind the quarry they had left so suddenly an hour before, Tom decided that before they went back to the coach, he would like to try a turn at the steering himself. It was such an incredible machine. It was a shame in a way, he added, that they wouldn't be able to keep it.

'What do you mean?' Geoff leant over the side to pick up Tom's rucksack from the quarry's edge. 'Why shouldn't we keep it?'

'Well . . . we can't, can we?' It was so obvious that Tom found the reason difficult to put into words. 'For a start, it's not ours.'

'Yes, it is. We found it.'

'That doesn't mean it belongs to us.'

'We know who it belongs to,' said Geoff. He pointed to the bottom of the quarry. 'He's down there and he doesn't want it any more.'

'That doesn't make any difference!' Tom looked

at his friend. 'Come on, Geoff. Your mum doesn't let you ride a bike on the main road – you think she'll let you buzz around town in something like this? You think *anyone* will?'

They were hovering directly over the cave. Beneath them, the Roman soldier stared out in front of him, as he had for the last millennium and a half.

'So when we get back, we just hand it over and . . . never see it again?'

'I wouldn't have thought so.'

'They'll take it away . . .'

'Yes.'

'We'll never have another chance to fly it . . .'

'No.'

'Or find out what any of these other buttons do . . .'

'No.'

'No . . .'

There was a long pause as an idea slowly grew in Geoff's mind. A very simple idea.

'I have a suggestion,' he said.

Miss Taylor strode up to the Hall with the thunder clouds almost visible above her head. She had spent the last forty minutes fruitlessly walking and calling through the woods and was in the mood to pull the arms off any child who dared so much as talk back to her.

'They're here.' Mr Urquart came down the path to meet her. 'Back ten minutes ago.'

'Right.' Miss Taylor's eyes narrowed. 'I want two ritual disembowelling knives and a sharpening stone . . .'

'I think I ought to warn you, they could both be in shock,' said Mr Urquart. 'They've been through a very traumatic experience.'

'It's nothing to the experience they're going to have when I . . .' Miss Taylor stopped. 'Why? What happened?'

'They found a body. A dead body.' Mr Urquart shook his head. 'I'm just hoping it doesn't leave them emotionally scarred.'

Miss Taylor looked up the hill to where the two boys were surrounded by an eager group of class-mates. Tom was holding a skull, and Geoff was moving the lower jaw like a ventriloquist's dummy to make it tell a 'Knock Knock' joke.

She walked briskly towards them, scattering small children on either side like leaves.

'Give me that.' Miss Taylor held out a hand.

As Geoff passed the skull across to her, a large spider crawled out of one of the eye sockets and one of the Year Nine's fainted.

'Pick her up, somebody.' Miss Taylor sighed and turned to Mr Urquart. 'Call the police, will you, Graham? And you –' she turned back to the boys – 'had better show me where you found this.'

It was astonishing, Geoff thought, how many people you needed just to decide what to do with a few bones. At the moment, he could count at least fourteen vehicles and more than thirty people, not including himself, Tom or Miss Taylor, gathered at the base of the quarry.

There were four policemen in two police cars, an ambulance with a nurse and two paramedics, a doctor and his wife, and a Land Rover and two cars containing the five-man team that had come out from the County Archaeology Department. Another Land Rover belonged to the farmer who owned the land, there was a van belonging to a representative of the local Wildlife Protection Society, and a Mini that had somehow contained six large men from the Cave Rescue Services.

The woman in charge of the archaeological team had short cropped hair, a silver ring in her nose, and was called Doctor Warner. She climbed out of the cave, brushing the worst of the dirt from clothes that had not been particularly clean when she went down.

'Definitely Roman,' she announced. 'Probably late third or early fourth century – it's difficult to tell at this stage – but he's been there at least fifteen hundred years.'

'Any idea how he died?' someone asked.

'Not really.' Doctor Warner shook her head. 'There are fifteen empty jars of Cypriot wine down there that might have something to do with it. Or he could have been poisoned by someone from the Free Britain Movement.' She paused. 'He was sealed in there when the roof of the cave collapsed, but that could have happened at any time.'

'So you don't know why he was down there?' asked Geoff.

'No.' The archaeologist looked thoughtfully back down at the body. 'He's a long way from the cave entrance, though. And in full armour. It's curious . . .'

'Romans didn't have machines, did they?' Tom blushed as everyone turned to look at him. 'I just wondered how he carried all the wine down there.'

Miss Taylor watched as Doctor Warner explained to Tom how Roman society was powered by slaves rather than technology, and felt a faint doubt stir in her mind. There was something not quite right in all this. She couldn't quite put her finger on what it was, but something about the way those boys were behaving didn't fit.

'They're asking questions, aren't they?' said Mr Urquart, standing beside her.

'What?'

'That archaeologist. They're asking her things. They don't usually do that, do they?'

Miss Taylor suddenly realized he was right. Tom and Geoff never asked questions. Questions got you noticed, and they had both spent years perfecting the technique of sitting at the back of a class attracting as little attention as possible. Attention might mean you had to do some work.

'It's like they are . . . interested,' Mr Urquart went on. 'I've never seen them like that before.'

'No,' said Miss Taylor, thoughtfully. 'Neither have I.'

As the school coach left the National Trust car park, Tom and Geoff sat together in seats near the back. Tom had the map from his worksheet spread out on his lap, and the two boys gazed intently out of the window as the coach turned out on to the road that would take them back to Stavely.

Mr Urquart, sitting at the front, caught a glimpse of them in the rear-view mirror and considered, not for the first time, what an odd pair they made. They were such different boys, in the way they looked as much as the way they behaved, and yet he knew that, in school and out, they were virtually inseparable. It was, most people agreed, a curious friendship.

He would have been even more puzzled if he had known what the boys were doing. Neither of them spoke as the coach set off down the road, but both stared intently out of the window at an isolated barn just visible at the top of the hill on their right.

It was a very ordinary barn, with open sides, of the sort farmers use to store bales of straw through the winter, but its location had been carefully marked on Tom's map. If Mr Urquart had seen it, he would have been impressed at the care that had been taken to note its exact position, and the way the boys now double-checked to make certain there had been no mistake.

Tom and Geoff wanted to be quite sure they could find it again, when they came back.

CHAPTER THREE

'As I see it,' Geoff said, pushing open the doors to the school library, 'we have two real problems. First, we have to get out there so we can fly it back. And second, we have to have somewhere ready to hide it when we do.'

As he followed his friend over to the desk, Tom privately thought they could have a good many more than two problems, but he said nothing. There seemed to be quite enough difficulties connected with the ones Geoff had mentioned.

Mr Urquart was on duty at the desk, signing out the books people wanted to borrow and he looked up at the boys in some surprise. He had never seen Tom or Geoff in the library before, and if what Miss Taylor had told him was true, there was some doubt whether either of them could read.

'Have you got any maps?' asked Geoff.

'Maps . . .' Mr Urquart carefully disguised his

surprise and stood up. 'I think we might be able to help. If you'd like to follow me?' And he led the way over to the reference section.

When he came back to the desk, Miss Taylor was waiting for him.

'What are those two doing in here?' She had lowered her voice until it sounded no louder than the rumble of passing lorries, and was staring suspiciously at Tom and Geoff.

'They wanted a map of our route yesterday,' Mr Urquart explained. 'I'm not sure, but I think they may be planning to go back.'

'You mean to the cave?'

'Yes. It's rather encouraging, isn't it?' Mr Urquart smiled happily at the boys, who were busily thumbing through the *Road Guide to Britain* he had given them. 'It really seems to have caught their imagination.'

Miss Taylor did not reply. Through narrowed eyes, she continued to stare at the boys.

'I wonder why they go around together all the time,' said Mr Urquart. 'I mean, as far as I can see, they've got nothing in common at all.'

'Are you doing anything on Saturday?'

'I'm sorry?' Mr Urquart blinked.

'Saturday,' Miss Taylor repeated. 'Didn't you say you had to go back out to the Park sometime, to make sure the next field trip wasn't anywhere near a quarry?'

'Yes. Well, I thought that sometime, I should –'

'If you went out there on Saturday,' said Miss Taylor, 'you could take the boys with you, couldn't you? Keep an eye on them. Maybe find out what's going on.'

'You think they're up to something?' asked Mr Urquart.

'I know they're up to something,' said Miss Taylor. 'I just want to know what it is.'

She paused for a moment to confiscate a Walkman from a passing sixteen-year-old.

'And you're quite wrong.'

Mr Urquart didn't always find it easy to keep track of conversations with Miss Taylor.

'About them.' The Deputy Head nodded towards Tom and Geoff. 'They have one thing in common.'

'They do?'

'They both come bottom of the class. Always have done. Ever since primary school.' Miss Taylor landed a meaty hand on Mr Urquart's shoulder. 'Take my word, it can be a very powerful bond.'

Tom carefully measured the distance with his ruler, but it only confirmed what he already suspected.

'It's not going to work,' he said. 'It's too far.'

According to the map, it was nearly fifty miles from Stavely to the barn where they had left Aquila. They would never be able to cycle that far in an afternoon.

'So . . . we have to think of something else.' Geoff sat back in his chair and stared at the ceiling.

'There isn't anything else,' said Tom. 'That's it. We've tried everything.'

He had a point. Cycling had not been the first possibility on their list. The evening before, Geoff had asked his parents if they could drive him out, but the answer had been no. Mr and Mrs Reynolds ran a newsagents that was open twelve hours a day, seven days a week, and they simply didn't have the time.

Tom's mother was in no position to help either. Mrs Baxter suffered from an illness called agoraphobia, which meant she was frightened of open spaces and couldn't go out of doors.

Geoff had rung the railway station, but trains do not run in National Parks, and the man at the bus depot had told him that no buses went within five miles of where they wanted to go. Cycling had been the only idea they had left.

Geoff was still trying to come up with an alternative when he looked up to see Mr Urquart standing at the end of the table.

'I don't know if it's of any interest,' said the teacher, 'but I'm going back out to the National Park on Saturday, and if either of you wanted to come with me . . .' He stopped, a little unnerved at the way the boys seemed to be staring at him.

'It's not compulsory or anything,' he added. 'It was just . . . you know, if you were interested.'

'I think we might be interested,' said Geoff. He smiled triumphantly as Mr Urquart walked back to his desk.

'There you are. Problem solved.'

Tom pointed out that there was still one difficulty.

'He'll know, won't he?'

'What?'

'Mr Urquart. If he takes us out to the site, he'll expect to take us back.'

'So?'

'But if we've flown home with Aquila, we won't be there for him to take back, will we? So he'll know something's happened, won't he?'

Geoff thought about it. Tom was right.

Could be a tricky one that . . .

Geoff worried about the problem all afternoon. He thought about it through Miss Poulson's history lesson on the causes of the First World War, and then through Mr Duncan's double maths. Nothing that either teacher said disturbed his train of thought and finally, on the way home, the answer came to him. It was a clever idea, and if Miss Poulson or Mr Duncan had heard it, they would have found it hard to believe that Geoff was its author.

'Supposing only one of us went with Mr Urquart on Saturday,' he suggested, as they turned into the street where Tom lived. 'And the other one stayed here.'

Tom grunted. He was looking at a stone he had found in the road just outside the school gates. He

28

couldn't be certain till he got it home, but he was pretty sure it was a piece of fluorite.

'Then at lunchtime, the one of us out there could say he wants to go for a walk, go up to the barn, get Aquila and fly it back here.'

If it was fluorite, thought Tom, it was remarkably pure. The crystal was almost colourless.

'Then whoever's back here gets in it, we both fly out to the site, whoever was out there before gets out, and whoever was back here flies it back. You see? We'll both be back where we're supposed to be. And Aquila will be in there.'

Geoff pointed to the garage at the top of Tom's drive.

'It's the perfect place to hide it. Your mum'll never see it. She never goes out.'

Tom stared at his friend as the idea slowly penetrated his brain. One of them would go out to the site on Saturday with Mr Urquart. In the course of the day, that person would fly Aquila back to Stavely, pick up the other one, they would both fly back out to the site, and then the one who'd been picked up would fly Aquila back to Stavely . . .

'No.' Tom shook his head, firmly. 'It wouldn't work.'

'What do you mean it wouldn't work? Of course it'd work. Why wouldn't it work? Tell me one thing about it that wouldn't work.' Geoff looked closely at Tom. 'You're not frightened, are you?'

Tom said nothing.

'I mean, there's nothing to be scared of, is there?'

'Nothing to be scared of?' Tom spoke with a sudden and surprising force. 'How about flying fifty miles in a machine we've only sat in twice that you found in a hole in the ground?'

'Oh, come on!' Geoff was slightly taken aback by the vehemence in Tom's voice. 'It'd be worth it, wouldn't it? To have something like that parked in there . . .'

'And what if it breaks down?' Tom's voice rose another notch. 'Or we get lost? Or if I bump into something, like a tree, or a small hill? Or a big hill? And we kill ourselves? Would it still be worth it?'

'You won't bump into anything,' said Geoff, and then remembered that the only time Tom had taken the controls, on the way up to the barn, he had bumped into a wall. 'I'll explain it all to you,' he added. 'It's really easy. You saw! I learnt in two minutes!'

'You learnt to swim in two minutes,' said Tom. 'You're that sort of person. I'm the one who had lessons for two years and still wears armbands, remember?'

Geoff stared at his friend. He hadn't seen Tom this determined since the time he had refused to go on the Death Slide at the American Theme Park.

'Look, all you have to do –'

'No.' Tom turned and started walking up the path to the back door. 'No, I'm sorry. I can't do it. You'll have to work out something else.'

And before Geoff could reply, Tom had gone into the house and closed the door.

In his bedroom that evening, Tom sat at his desk relabelling his collection of rocks. He had always collected rocks. His mother said it had started when he was three and found a tiny fire opal on the beach in the days when they still went on holiday – and he had been collecting ever since. She had no idea why, though privately she suspected that rocks went at about the right speed for Tom. There was something about the pace of life of a lump of granite that suited him.

And it was true that Tom always turned to his collection whenever he had a problem or the smooth surface of life became disturbed. He had found there was something soothing in the feel of a piece of agate as you ran it through your fingers, something steadying and calming in the idea that it had been that shape for four million years, something quietly reassuring in its patient, glinting stillness.

But at the moment, Tom was finding it difficult to concentrate on colour-coding his mineral deposits. Thoughts of Geoff and Aquila filled his mind.

A part of him wanted very much to do as Geoff had suggested, and not just because Geoff was his friend. Aquila, he knew, was not the sort of discovery one made every day, and the longer it was left in the barn, the more likely it was that someone else would find it.

Geoff's idea would work. It was what Tom wanted to do, it was right, it was what he'd like . . . But when Geoff had asked Tom if he was frightened, he had not understood his friend at all. Frightened did not begin to describe the stomach-churning, mind-numbing sensation that took over Tom's body at the thought of flying Aquila on his own. He had been trying desperately to think of some other way they might be able to bring it home, but with no success.

His mother appeared at the door with a plate of biscuits and a mug of hot chocolate. Mrs Baxter was a small, nervous woman with a worried look on her face. A lot of things worried Mrs Baxter, but at the moment she was worrying particularly about Tom. She was worried that she had upset him when she said she could not take him out to see the body of the Roman centurion in his cave. She had been worrying about it all day.

'I'm sorry about Saturday,' she said. 'But you do understand, don't you?'

'Yes, of course.' Tom picked up his mug. 'And it doesn't matter. Mr Urquart said he'd take us.'

'The Geography teacher?'

Tom nodded. 'But I think I've changed my mind anyway. I'm not sure I want to go.'

Mrs Baxter looked, if possible, even more worried.

'It's my fault, isn't it?' she said. 'You'd want to go if it was me taking you, and it's what I ought to be doing. I'm your mother.'

'I told you, it doesn't matter,' said Tom. 'Really. It's all right.'

'It is not all right. And it does matter.' Mrs Baxter sniffed and took out a handkerchief. 'It's silly not to do something you want to do – that's right to do, that you'd like to do – just because you're too frightened. It's stupid. And it's wrong.'

She blew her nose sharply. 'Don't forget to bring your mug down when you've finished.' She picked up the empty tray and took it back downstairs.

Tom stared at the door for some moments after she had gone. Then, slowly, he picked up the mobile phone his mother had given him for calling the police in an emergency, and dialled a number.

Mrs Reynolds answered. She said Geoff had gone out for a walk, but asked if she could take a message.

'If you could tell him', said Tom, 'that I've changed my mind, and it's OK about Saturday. He'll understand.'

He put down the phone, then got out an exercise book and his pen, and started to write. Carefully, he began to describe exactly what had happened when they had found Aquila, and how they were planning to bring it home.

If he was killed on Saturday, and he was fairly sure that he would be, it seemed only fair that his mother should have a chance of knowing the truth.

CHAPTER FOUR

Miss Poulson, the History teacher, was discussing the difficulties of trench warfare, and had begun to explain the importance of air reconnaissance, when her voice trailed off into silence.

She had just seen that Geoff Reynolds had his hand up.

'I was wondering', he asked, 'if you knew how the pilots found their way around then. If they didn't have radar and things.'

For a moment, Miss Poulson was too astonished to speak. She could hardly have been more surprised if the radiator had stepped away from the wall and casually announced it wanted to stand somewhere else. Geoff never spoke in class, unless you asked him a direct question, and sometimes not then.

'I'm sorry?' she asked.

'How they knew how to get to anywhere,' Geoff

repeated, patiently. 'The pilots. Without instruments.'

Miss Poulson quickly recovered and gave the class a brief lecture on the early techniques of air navigation.

'They followed the natural features of the land, you see,' she explained. 'With a map and a compass they could follow the roads, the rivers, and the railway lines. They could use the landmarks, like churches and castles, and of course, if they got lost they could always land in a field and look at a signpost or something. Though, as a matter of fact, the air ace Von Richtofen once said that with a map and a compass, it was actually more difficult to get lost in the air than it was on land.'

She was quite touched, as she later told her colleagues, at how grateful Geoff had been for the information, and how his friend Tom had actually asked her to speak more slowly, so that he had time to make proper notes.

Mr Urquart was one of the little circle that had gathered in the staffroom to hear her extraordinary story, and he decided he might mention it to Miss Taylor.

He had a feeling she would be interested.

On their way home after school, the boys bought a compass from Millet's, and a large *Road Atlas of Great Britain* from Smith's. Sitting in Tom's bedroom, they carefully began working out their route.

'The last bit's going to be the trickiest,' said Geoff. 'Coming down and landing in your garden. That's when we're most likely to be seen. The only way is to do it fast. Faster the better. I think it'd better be me.' He took another biscuit from the plate Mrs Baxter had provided. 'Which means you'd better go out with Mr Urquart and do the first leg.'

'You think I should go first?' Tom had not had a great deal of sleep the night before. His face was pale, and he had developed a nervous tic in the cheek under his right eye. 'On my own?'

'It's probably best.' Geoff was still studying the map. 'I mean, if there's any problem with navigating and things, at least you can come down and check a signpost.'

Geoff himself would not be able to check any signposts. As Miss Taylor had rightly assessed, Geoff could not read. He was one of those unfortunate people who, when presented with a word like 'lemon' sometimes see it as 'melon', sometimes as 'nomel' and only occasionally as 'lemon'. It can make learning to read a confusing process, and Geoff had long since abandoned any serious attempt at doing it.

'Tomorrow, we'll find a quiet place outside town where you can pick me up. One of those fields behind the station might be good.'

Geoff took another biscuit, and then realized it was the last and that Tom had not yet had any.

'I'm not very hungry,' said Tom. 'You go ahead.'

Geoff looked closely at his friend. 'You're quite sure this is all right?'

'Oh, definitely.' Tom nodded vigorously. 'Absolutely fine.' His cheek twitched violently a couple of times.

'I mean, if you don't want to do it, you can always change your mind.'

'Not a chance.' The half of Tom's face that wasn't twitching gave a good impression of a smile. 'No, no. Looking forward to it. It'll be . . . an adventure.'

Before Geoff could reply, Mrs Baxter came in to say it was time he went home. She wanted Tom to get to bed early that night. She thought he needed to catch up on his sleep.

On Friday, they gathered together all the things Tom would need for the journey. In a backpack they put the road atlas, the compass, the mobile phone, one of the first-aid kits from Tom's bathroom, some chocolate, a piece of rope so Tom could tie himself to the seat so he did not fall out, and a second map he had bought in case the first one blew away in the wind.

Both boys learned the route they would take until they knew it backwards. They needed to know it backwards, of course, as they were travelling both ways. And then after school, they cycled out to check the exact spot in the field behind the station where Geoff would be waiting for Tom to pick him up.

By the time he got home that evening, the twitch

in Tom's cheek had become so violent that it was difficult to drink his hot chocolate without spilling it. Mrs Baxter was quite concerned and asked if he was feeling ill. Tom assured her that he had never felt better, but by Saturday morning when Mr Urquart arrived, on top of the twitching, he had developed a slight stammer.

'Frankly, I'm worried about him,' Mrs Baxter admitted. 'I've told him he ought to stay in bed, but he won't hear of it. He's been so looking forward to going out with you.'

'I'm O-K-K-K,' said Tom. 'Really. I'm f-fine.'

'Perhaps he's getting the same thing as Geoff Reynolds,' said Mr Urquart. 'He rang me this morning saying he can't come today. Apparently he's got a stomach virus.'

Mrs Baxter looked doubtfully at Tom. 'Maybe you should stay at home,' she said. 'You haven't had any breakfast, and you look awful.'

'I'm fine!' Tom insisted. 'You can't k-keep me at home today. You just c-c-can't.'

Mr Urquart rather admired his determination.

'Don't worry, Mrs Baxter.' He smiled reassuringly. 'I'll bring him straight home if there's any problem.' He turned to Tom. 'Come on then. Let's go.'

Tom picked up his bag and followed the teacher down the drive, his head twitching rhythmically as they went.

Mrs Baxter, of course, did not come out to the

car. She stayed indoors and waved goodbye from the window.

The site at the quarry looked very different from the day that Tom and Geoff had fallen into it.

Most of the undergrowth had been cleared. Poles and tapes criss-crossed the ground in neat squares. To one side a row of tents had been erected along with two caravans and some Portaloos, and the entrance to the cave where they had found the skeleton was now covered in polythene sheeting, wrapped round scaffolding to protect it from the weather.

Doctor Warner came over to meet them as they climbed out of the car. She was wearing a denim waistcoat which showed a tattoo on each shoulder, and her hair was a different colour, but she greeted them warmly and insisted on showing them round herself.

In one of the tents, the skeleton of the Roman soldier lay stretched out on a table with his armour beside him.

'We've established he was a centurion of the twentieth legion,' she explained. 'And the coins we've found, as well as the details of the armour, mean he probably died somewhere towards the end of the third century.'

Mr Urquart asked if they had any idea how he had died.

'We think it was an accident.' Doctor Warner gave the skull an affectionate rap with her knuckles. 'I don't know if you noticed the type of rock in the cave . . .'

'Carboniferous l-limestone,' said Tom.

Mr Urquart gave him an odd look, but Doctor Warner only nodded approvingly.

'Precisely. The tunnel was the shaft of a lead mine, and as far as we can see, he just happened to be in there when the roof collapsed.'

'You mean he s-suffocated?'

Doctor Warner nodded. 'The odd thing is, the mine was worked out at least a hundred years before. So we're a little puzzled as to why our man was down there.'

'Perhaps he was hiding something,' Mr Urquart suggested. 'Something he didn't want anyone else to find.'

'If he was, we haven't found it yet.' Doctor Warner led them over to another table. 'All we've dug up so far are these.' She pointed to a large collection of amphorae that had, she explained, once contained wine from all corners of the Empire.

'And there's this, of course,' she added, moving to the end of the table and picking up a collection of leather straps joined by a series of buckles and clips. 'We're not sure what it is, but my theory is that it's a safety harness. You know, to stop a Roman pilot falling out of his jet when he's looping the loop.'

Mr Urquart was the first to realize she was joking, and laughed politely.

40

'It has a neat inscription.' Doctor Warner ran her fingers over the letters cut into one of the leather cross straps. '*Licet volare si in tergo aquilae volat.*'

'Aquila?' Tom looked up. 'W-what does that mean?'

'An eagle,' said Doctor Warner. 'It's an old Latin proverb. "A man can fly where he will, if he rides on the back of an eagle." Now . . .' She put down the harness. 'How about some lunch and then I'll show you the cave.'

Mr Urquart looked at his watch and explained that he didn't really have time for lunch. As he had told the boys, his main reason for coming out to the site was so that he could find some alternative locations for his next geography field trip.

'I'll be back about two,' he told Tom. 'You're sure you'll be all right here till then?'

'F-fine,' said Tom, his face twitching violently. 'No p-problem at all.'

When Mr Urquart had left, Tom asked Doctor Warner if she would mind if he went for a walk. What he would have done if she said yes, he had no idea, but she made no objection.

'Sure, go ahead.' She gave him a smile. 'But be careful. People fall down holes in the ground around here.'

Aquila was still there.

Carefully, Tom pulled aside the bales of straw that

had covered it, climbed inside, and then sat for a moment watching as the lights blinked into life.

He opened his backpack, took out the rope and looped it under his seat before tying the ends firmly round his waist. Then he took out the compass, the road map, the telephone, a small piece of paper and some Sellotape.

The paper was a drawing of the four blue lights, shaped liked a flower. On each of the quarters, Tom had written a reminder of what pressing that particular button would do – 'Forward', 'Back', 'Up' and 'Down' – and now he carefully taped the picture to the dashboard, alongside the real thing. He kept the compass in his lap, and put the map and the telephone on the seat beside him.

Carefully reaching out, he put the tip of his finger on the button that his diagram said meant 'Forward'. Gently he pushed, and Aquila floated forward, light as a thistledown, out of the barn, into the sunshine.

The hills and grassland of the Peak District were spread out before him, but Tom was not in the mood to admire scenery. The next thing was to go up. He moved his finger to the button at the top, pushed, and Aquila rose silently through the air. There was no real sensation of movement. If Tom had had his eyes closed, he would barely have been aware that he was moving at all, but when he looked over the side he saw a tractor that seemed no bigger than a spot of paint, travelling across a field below him.

'Go high,' Geoff had said. 'If the cars look like little dots, then that's what you'll look like to them.'

It seemed high enough. Tom took up the compass, found east, and pulled on the handle with his right hand to swing Aquila round. It was as he reached out to push the forward button again that he realized the strangest thing had happened.

He was not frightened any more.

It was an almost perfect flight. Tom had been travelling for only a few minutes before he realized he could see his first landmark, the six-lane ribbon of the motorway, directly ahead. When he was above it, he stopped, swung Aquila round to the left, and followed the road north until he saw the unmistakable pattern of a junction. He stopped again, turned east, and tracked what, according to his map, was the A617 to Southwell.

A large town passed below him at a point where the map said he ought to be flying over Mansfield. Shortly after that, Sherwood Forest went by just where it was supposed to be, and then he saw the railway, cutting across the countryside ahead as clearly as a line on a piece of paper. A goods train was heading north, and Tom turned to follow it the last dozen miles to home.

His only mistake was deciding to double-check his position by going down to look at a road sign. Knowing that all road turnings have signposts, he took Aquila down to a junction to look at one – and found that everything was just as it should be. According to the sign, Stavely was seven miles ahead, and he was about to take Aquila back up when he heard the sound of an approaching car.

Anxious not to be seen, Tom hurriedly pushed the 'Up' button, but unfortunately hit the 'Back' button at the same time, with the result that Aquila shot backwards and upwards at an angle of forty-five degrees, taking a set of telephone cables and three telegraph poles as it went.

At about 150 metres, the wires and the trailing poles slid off the back of Aquila and plummeted casually back to earth like a set of darts. Tom, peering over the side, was relieved to see them land among some trees instead of in the road.

Two minutes later, he was bringing Aquila down in the field behind Stavely station and coasting over the grass to where an ecstatic Geoff was waiting.

'Fantastic! You did it!' Geoff punched him happily on the shoulder. 'No problems or anything?'

'Not really,' said Tom. 'Nothing worth mentioning.'

Geoff took the controls for the journey back. With Tom map-reading, they flew south down the railway line to Penton Castle, and turned right. They followed the road back through Sherwood Forest and Mansfield to the motorway, turned south again, and finally due west, to bring themselves back to the Park. When Geoff dropped Tom off by the barn, they found the whole journey had taken a little under twelve minutes.

Ten minutes after that, Tom was back with Doctor Warner and when Mr Urquart returned, he found the two of them in the canteen tent discussing how the Romans might have gone about extracting lead ore from limestone.

'Smart boy that,' the archaeologist commented, as she walked with Mr Urquart to his car. 'Must be fun having someone like that in your class.'

'Yes, it's very . . . stimulating.' Mr Urquart hesitated. 'Can I ask . . . You didn't have any trouble getting him to talk?'

'Trouble!' Doctor Warner laughed. 'I don't think he's stopped since he got back from his walk. Except to eat of course.'

She looked across to the canteen tent, where Tom was finishing what had to be his fourth pizza. 'You forget how much they can tuck away at that age, don't you?'

'What did he talk about?'

'All sorts of things really. He was asking lots of questions about Roman technology to start with. You know, whether they knew about electricity, that sort of thing. Then we got on to flying for some reason. But mostly, of course, we've been discussing rocks.' She shook her head in admiration. 'Not many boys his age know that much geology. Surprised me.'

'Yes,' said Mr Urquart thoughtfully. 'It can

surprise a lot of people. I'm very grateful to you.'

'Grateful?'

'Well, coming out here's obviously done him a lot of good.' Mr Urquart looked at Tom as he walked over to the car. There was a smile on his face, no trace of a twitch, and even his stammer seemed to have disappeared.

'Are you sure all you did was talk to him?'

'Talk and eat,' said Doctor Warner. 'I promise you, that's all he's done since he got here.'

Mr Urquart thanked her again, climbed into his car, and wondered what on earth he was going to tell Miss Taylor.

When Tom got home, Mrs Baxter told him that Geoff was out in the garage, and wanted to see him.

'He's been out there for hours waiting for you to come back,' she said. 'Apparently, he's got something to show you.'

In the garage, Tom found Geoff sitting in Aquila. He had washed off all the bits of mud that had stuck to the hull in the cave, and carefully swept out the bits of loose straw that had got into the cockpit while it was in the barn.

He had also stuck a couple of go-fast stickers down each side and another one on the back that said 'My other car's a Ferrari.'

He climbed out when Tom appeared, and for some minutes the two boys simply stood there together and stared at it.

'You got back all right, then?' asked Tom eventually. 'No one saw you?'

'I don't think so.' Geoff reached out and stroked a hand along the upward curve of Aquila's bow, then ran it along to the bottom of one of the gold letters.

'I wonder why it's called Aquila?'

'It means an eagle,' said Tom.

'An eagle?'

Tom nodded. 'A man can fly anywhere, if he rides on the back of an eagle.'

'Too right,' said Geoff, softly. 'Too right.'

CHAPTER FIVE

The front page of the *Sunday Mirror* next morning came as something of a shock to both boys.

Geoff was helping his father put out the papers in the shop, when he saw the set of 'exclusive' pictures of a UFO spotted seven miles south of Stavely, all over the front page. Aquila's shape, with Tom inside, was clearly recognizable.

He showed the paper to his father, who read the article aloud in between serving customers. Mr Reynolds had long believed that the earth was being visited by aliens from space, and the story confirmed his theory that they were up to no good in the process.

According to the newspaper, a birdwatcher called Brian Bovis had seen a strange machine fly down and hover in the air at a road junction outside Halterworth. From his hiding place in the woods, he had hurriedly lined up his camera for a picture, only to see the alien craft shoot up into the air where, using what Mr Bovis described as 'some sort of power beam', it had rooted out a row of telegraph poles and sent them hurtling back to earth in an obvious attempt to kill him before he could tell anyone what he had seen.

On the inside pages of the paper, there were more pictures. One was of the telegraph pole which had landed in the earth centimetres from where Mr Bovis had been standing and another, fifty metres away, had speared his motorcycle to the ground like a cocktail sausage.

The photos of Aquila were rather blurred as Mr Bovis' camera had unfortunately been focused to take close-ups of a feeding hedge-warbler, but you could just make out the small head and big dark eyes of the alien creature that sat inside.

'Wouldn't like to meet him on a dark night.' Mr Reynolds studied the photo closely. 'Nasty piece of work that.' He passed the paper back to Geoff and went off to serve another customer. After breakfast, Geoff took it round to show Tom.

'You never said anything about telegraph poles and a power beam,' he said. 'How did you do it?'

Tom did not reply. As it happened, he had some rather alarming news of his own. The police had come to his house early that morning to ask Mrs Baxter if she had seen any flying saucers in her garden recently.

'Flying saucers?' The look of worry on Mrs Baxter's face deepened. 'What do you mean?'

'We had some reports yesterday about something in the sky,' the sergeant explained. 'And then a phone call from someone who says they saw it land on your lawn.'

'You're saying somebody saw me land?' said Geoff, when Tom told him about it.

'Yes, but it might be all right. It was only Mrs Murphy.'

Mrs Murphy was the old lady who lived on her own in the house next door to Tom's.

'They got the doctor round, and he said it was probably a side effect of this new medicine she's been taking for her depression.'

'So nobody believed her?'

Tom shook his head. 'I don't think so. But it might be safest if we kept Aquila indoors for a few days. At least in the daytime.'

It was disappointing, but Geoff had to agree it was the only sensible thing to do.

Sitting in the garage, he gently floated Aquila a few metres up and down and side to side, while Tom read the article in the *Sunday Mirror*.

According to the paper, the damage to the tele-phone lines was estimated at hundreds of pounds, and when Tom looked at the pictures, he couldn't help thinking that if the telegraph poles had fallen even a fraction further to the left . . .

'I tell you what.' Geoff took out his chewing gum

and stuck it on the dash. 'If we can't go outside or anything, we could find out what some of these do.' He gestured to the lights in front of him.

'How?' asked Tom.

'Well, we push a few and see what happens.'

'But we don't know what they'll do!'

'That's why I'm suggesting we push them,' Geoff explained patiently. 'So we'd know.'

'But that could be . . . dangerous.' Tom was still thinking about his near miss on the birdwatcher, and the skin under his right eye flickered faintly.

Geoff shrugged. 'I think it'd probably be all right. I mean, you wouldn't design something like this to kill whoever was inside it, would you?'

'I don't know,' said Tom. 'But I . . .' He stopped. 'Are we going forwards?'

Geoff leaned over the side to peer at the floor and found Aquila was, very slowly, floating towards the door. He looked at the dashboard and saw his chewing gum had dribbled down over the forward control. He peeled it off, and flicked the button back out with his fingernail.

'I tell you what. We'll just try one of them. I mean, one wouldn't do any harm, would it?'

Tom was not entirely convinced by this.

'It's just to see what happens.' Geoff put the chewing gum back in his mouth. 'We'll probably find it turns on the heater or something.' He pointed to a small blue light in the far corner. 'This one looks pretty harmless. Let's try that.' And before Tom could say anything, Geoff reached out a thumb and pressed firmly at the light.

Nothing happened.

The boys looked round, and Geoff pressed again. There was a faint smell in the air that Tom couldn't quite place, but otherwise nothing had changed. His relief mingled with a slight sense of disappointment.

'OK, I'll try this one.' Geoff reached out a finger to a larger disc in the centre of the dashboard that glowed a luminescent yellow.

'I thought you said one button.'

'One button that works!' protested Geoff. 'There's not much point doing it unless we find one that works, is there? Where are you going?'

Tom was climbing out of Aquila. 'I'm sorry,' he said firmly. 'If you want to risk getting killed, you can do it on your own. I'm going over here. Out of the way.'

He went to stand by the wall at the back of the garage, his arms folded.

'Honestly, I don't know what you're worrying about.' Geoff shook his head. 'Nothing's going to happen.' He gave Tom a brief smile, pressed down with his finger . . .

. . . and both he and Aquila disappeared.

Standing at the sink in the kitchen, peeling potatoes, Mrs Baxter was worrying about her neighbour, Mrs Murphy. The old lady had not been in good health for some time. She was lonely, she had trouble with her legs, and now she was seeing spaceships land in the garden.

Some years before, when Mrs Baxter had first moved to Stavely, Mrs Murphy's kindness had helped her through a difficult time. Now, it seemed, she was in need of help herself, and Mrs Baxter would have liked very much to give it. She would have liked to call round, to ask if she could help with the shopping, to sit down and talk over a coffee . . . but she couldn't.

Mrs Baxter's agoraphobia had started as nothing more than a vague reluctance to go out of the house. She had found she disliked being in crowds, that travelling on public transport made her nervous, and that she only felt really comfortable and secure in the privacy of her own home. Over the months, the reluctance to leave had become stronger until now the truth was that she had not set so much as a foot outside her house for nearly three years. Anything she needed, she ordered over the phone or from catalogues and Tom collected any items that could not be delivered. It was an arrangement that had seemed largely satisfactory. Until now.

She could at least phone, Mrs Baxter thought, as she put the saucepan of potatoes on the cooker. She could ring and ask her neighbour how she was feeling and find out exactly what the doctor had said – and she was reaching for the phone when she noticed the garden fence was on fire.

Eager flames were licking hungrily up one of the

wooden panels at the bottom of the garden and as she watched, Mrs Baxter heard a dull, booming sound as Mrs Murphy's shed, just the other side of the fence, went up in a ball of fire.

With trembling fingers, she dialled 999 and asked for the fire brigade.

In the garage, it was very quiet. Tom stared at the emptiness around him with a sick feeling in his stomach.

'Geoff?' he called, weakly. 'What's happened?'

'I don't understand.' Geoff's disembodied voice came from somewhere in the middle of the room. 'It's got a light on. It must be there to do something.'

Tom looked round. Geoff's voice sounded perfectly normal, but there was no Geoff. There was nobody in the garage but himself.

'Geoff? Are you there?'

'I'll try it again . . .'

For a moment, Geoff and Aquila were back. Geoff, with a finger poised over the yellow button, looked disappointedly around.

'What a let-down!' He pressed the button again, and disappeared. 'I think I'll try another one.'

'Geoff!' Tom shouted from his place at the back of the garage. 'Please! Don't touch anything!'

Tom reached behind him and grabbed a spade that had been leaning against the back wall. He picked it up and stepped cautiously forwards.

'What . . . what are you doing?'

54

There was a note of concern in Geoff's voice, but Tom ignored him. Edging round to the side of where Aquila had been, he lifted the spade and let it fall. It stopped in mid-air with a clanging sound, a metre or so above the ground.

'Have you gone mad? You'll damage the paint.' Geoff stood up in Aquila and stared down at Tom. At least, Tom presumed he was standing up. All he could actually see was Geoff's body down to his waist. Below that, his legs and Aquila were still invisible.

'What do you think you're doing?'

By way of reply, Tom simply pointed, and Geoff looked down. For a moment he froze in astonishment, but then he reached down, dipping a hand into the emptiness. It disappeared. When he lifted the hand out, it was back again.

'Hang on a minute.' Geoff disappeared completely as he sat down, and a moment later both he and Aquila had reappeared. His finger was poised over the yellow light.

'You can see me now?'

'Yes.'

'And now I've gone again?'

'Right.'

'Oh, wow!' Aquila became visible again and Geoff's face was wreathed in smiles. 'Oh, wow! This . . . this is cool! You know what we have here?'

If Tom knew, he did not reply. He was staring thoughtfully at the spade he still held in his hand. In the centre, there was a small hole about two centimetres across and, judging by the dribbles of melted metal that had formed at its base, it had been made by something extremely hot.

He went to the back of the garage, to the place where the spade had been leaning against the wall, and knelt down. A few centimetres above the ground, he could see an identical circular hole drilled through the brickwork, its sides as smooth as glass. It went right through the wall, and he could see fronds of ivy on the other side, blowing in the wind.

'I don't believe this.' Geoff was half standing in an invisible Aquila, slowly bobbing up and down to watch his body vanish and then reappear. 'Just as well you stayed outside, isn't it?'

Tom was not really listening.

'I mean, if you hadn't stayed outside,' Geoff went on, 'we'd have just thought it was like the first button and didn't work at all . . .'

'I wouldn't be too sure of that.' Tom stood up.

'What?'

'About the first button not working.'

He held up the spade for Geoff to see and, as he did so, both boys caught the sound of fire engines getting closer.

There were eleven fires in all: four garden fences, Mrs Murphy's shed, a sunlounger, a tree, three bushes and a basket of washing. All of them were still vigorously burning when the fire brigade arrived.

The fire chief was understandably puzzled that eleven separate fires should have broken out in half a dozen gardens at exactly the same time, but he decided eventually that the fire in the garden shed must have started all the others. An exploding petrol can, he believed, had showered its contents over the fences to start the fires on either side.

It seemed plausible, and it was certainly a lot more plausible than Mrs Murphy's claim that the fires had been started by a laser-cannon from the spaceship she had seen the previous day. It was not an idea that anyone else took seriously, though it was curious, as a police constable pointed out, that all eleven fires were in an exact straight line.

'I think it might be best if we didn't try any more buttons for a while,' said Tom.

And for the moment, Geoff agreed.

That afternoon they took Aquila out on its first invisible flight around Stavely, and Geoff stopped over the park to perform a brief experiment. Hovering a couple of hundred metres above the lake with Aquila's nose pointing slightly downwards, Geoff stabbed briefly at the blue button again.

The beam of light that appeared from the back of Aquila was bright enough to dazzle, but what most impressed the boys was the way it seemed to go on and on and on. It was there for only a fraction of a second, but it seemed to stretch up into the sky for ever. Tom had the feeling that if it met a satellite

40,000 miles up, it would punch a neat two-centimetre hole through it as easily as it had through the garage wall.

They had, when he thought about it, been rather lucky. If Aquila had been pointing a different way, if the laser beam had shot through a row of houses instead of gardens, if it had gone through people instead of fences . . .

Geoff was less worried, and he was still curious about what the other lights on Aquila might do, but for now he was prepared to concede that it would be wiser, in the short term, not to conduct any more experiments.

What they already knew Aquila could do was exciting enough for the moment.

Mrs Baxter sat in her kitchen, and for once she was feeling not so much worried as angry. It was bad enough when you couldn't leave your house to go and help an old friend and neighbour, she thought, but when you couldn't even go outside with a bucket of water to try and stop your own property burning down, then . . .

. . . then it was time something was done.

Chapter Six

On Monday morning, the boys took Aquila to school. It was a journey which normally took them about fifteen minutes on foot, but the flight, with Geoff at the controls, was a matter of seconds.

In Aquila, there was no waiting to cross the road. There were no late buses and no traffic hold-ups. You simply took off into the air, pointed the nose to where you wanted to go, and went.

What did take time that first morning was finding somewhere in the school grounds to leave Aquila once they had got there. As it was invisible, you might have thought they could leave it wherever they wanted, but both Geoff and Tom had already realized that it was not quite that simple.

Although Aquila could not be seen, it was still there, and if it was left where someone might walk into it, its existence would hardly remain a secret very long. It had to be left where nobody went, and finding such a place was harder than you might think. There were plenty of places where people did not go very often, but nowhere the boys could be absolutely sure Aquila would be undisturbed.

Tom suggested leaving it above a flower bed, on the grounds that nobody walked on them, but Geoff pointed out that there were gardeners and, even as they talked, a tennis ball landed on the rose bed beneath them, and the boy who had thrown it naturally stepped out over the flowers to retrieve it.

Geoff's suggestion was that they leave Aquila high enough in the air for anyone walking around to be able to pass underneath it, but then the problem was how to get in and out. You could probably jump out all right, Tom said, but then you would need a ladder to be able to climb back in.

In the end, and with the bell already ringing for the start of school, they left it three metres in the air by a fire escape at the back of the domestic science block. It was on the edge of the school grounds, at the end of the playing field, and far enough away from most school activity for the boys to be reasonably confident of being able to retrieve it without being seen.

As they hurried over towards the main building, Geoff felt a certain satisfaction at the way they had solved the problem.

'It's the perfect place,' he said, contentedly. 'I think it'll be safe there.'

'Completely safe,' agreed Tom. 'Nothing to worry about at all.'

From her office window on the first floor, Miss Taylor watched as the two boys scurried into school. They had a cheerful, happy look that merely confirmed her suspicion that they were up to no good.

She swivelled round in her chair to face Mr Urquart.

'You have no idea what they were really doing?'

'As I said, I only took Tom in the end,' Mr Urquart explained. 'But he just seemed to be . . . interested in the site.'

'Hmm . . .' Miss Taylor thoughtfully fingered a thumbscrew on her desk. It had been a leaving present from the staff at her last school, and playing with it helped her think.

'Was he carrying anything when he went home?'

'Carrying?'

'Yes. It occurred to me', said Miss Taylor, 'that they might have found something out there while they were on your field trip, hidden it, and then gone back the second time, so they could bring it back.'

'Oh, I see.' Mr Urquart thought for a moment, but then shook his head. 'No. Tom had a backpack, but there was nothing in it. I remember he tipped everything out in the car on the way home, looking for food. I suppose he might have had something in his pockets, but if it was that small, he could have brought it back the first time, couldn't he?'

'Yes . . .' Miss Taylor spun the thumbscrew another couple of turns. 'And you say he talked to this woman about . . . geology?'

'That's what she told me.' Mr Urquart nodded decisively. 'She said he had a remarkable knowledge for a boy his age. I must admit I didn't think he'd recognize carboniferous limestone.'

'He's never shown any of this knowledge in class?'

'He's never shown *any* knowledge in class,' said Mr Urquart. 'I've never heard him talk.'

At break, Tom sat in a corner of the library with the *Encyclopedia of Flight* on the table in front of him, studying the entry on air safety. Geoff had gone off to get something to eat from the lunch boxes they had left in Aquila, and was probably taking a quick flight around town, but Tom had decided it was important that one of them do some basic research into the rules of the air. He was particularly anxious to avoid the sort of near-collision that had happened on their way home from the park the day before.

They had been flying high, 'breathing a bit of cloud' as Geoff put it, peacefully nibbling some ginger nuts, when an RAF Harrier GR7 had come storming towards them at something over 700 miles an hour.

Afterwards, they had realized the pilot could have had no idea they were there. They were, after all, invisible, but at the time it had felt like being run down by a train.

Geoff had dropped his biscuit, grabbed the controls and sent Aquila into a screaming dive as the bomber flew straight overhead, close enough for Tom to see the stencilled numbers on the missiles slung beneath its wings. By the time they had emerged below cloud level, the Harrier had gone, and showed no signs of reappearing, but it had been a distinctly unnerving experience.

Tom knew that all aircraft, military and civil, are only allowed to fly in particular areas and at regulated heights and he was hoping that the encyclopedia could tell him what these were so they could make sure Aquila was always somewhere else.

He was still reading the first paragraph, on the founding of the Civil Aviation Authority, when Geoff appeared beside him, his face white as a sheet. He had been running, and he was barely able to speak.

'It's gone!' he said, breathlessly.

'What's gone?'

'It,' hissed Geoff. 'It's gone!'

He gave up trying to talk, grabbed Tom's arm and pulled him out of the library. Together they ran out of the main building, along past the bike sheds, and round to the back of the domestic science block. They stopped under the fire-escape ladder and Geoff picked up a stick and gave it to Tom.

'Go on. Try it for yourself.'

Tom climbed a few steps up the ladder, and used the stick to poke the air where they had left Aquila.

There was nothing there.

'Did we leave it a bit higher?'

'I've been all the way to the top. It's no use. I'm telling you, it's gone.'

'But why . . . I mean, where . . . How?'

It was the question Geoff had been asking himself ever since he had discovered Aquila was no longer where they had left it, and he had a miserable feeling he knew the answer.

'I think it was the chewing gum.'

'What?'

'The bit of chewing gum that's stuck in the forward control. It's all right as long as you remember to flick the button back out when you stop, but this morning was such a rush . . .'

'You forgot?'

Geoff nodded. He couldn't bring himself to speak.

Together the two boys stared out across the playing field. An invisible Aquila was out there somewhere, moving further away with every passing second.

They were still wondering what to do about it as the bell rang for the end of break.

Miss Taylor caught Mr Urquart as he passed her office on the way to his classroom.

'He's been to the library again.'

'What?'

'Tom Baxter. He came in at the start of break and

took out some books.' Miss Taylor looked over the top of her glasses at a list in her hand. 'He got the *Encyclopedia of Flight, One Hundred Places of Interest to Visit in the Midlands*, and *The Invisible Man* by H. G. Wells.'

'Goodness,' said Mr Urquart. 'Why would he want them?'

'I'm going to ring his mother at lunchtime.' Miss Taylor headed back into her office. 'See if she can explain any of this.'

At the start of the lunch break, Tom and Geoff returned to the base of the fire escape where they had left Aquila and wondered how you set about finding something that was invisible.

They had to find it, Tom thought. Apart from anything else, they couldn't have any lunch until they did.

They knew roughly the direction Aquila must be moving. It had been left pointing out across the playing field, and they knew it was about three metres up in the air. Geoff's idea was that they start walking across the field with long sticks, waving them above their heads until they hit something solid. Unfortunately, it was the sort of thing that they knew would attract a certain amount of attention, particularly as the first eleven football team had just come out on the field for a practice.

Tom, who had been thinking about the problem all through double biology, had the glimmerings of a different idea.

'If it's moving like it did in the garage,' he said, 'it must be going very slowly. We know it's heading over there.' He pointed to the far side of the field. 'And if we were waiting for it by the trees when it got there, one of us could climb up and get back in.'

'But we don't know when it'll get to the trees, do we?' said Geoff. 'It could happen in the middle of the night, or sometime next week. We can't just stand there and wait for it.'

'What we have to do', said Tom, 'is calculate how fast it's going, and I thought . . .'

But Tom never got to say what it was that he thought. At that moment, someone kicked the ball from the far end of the field and a large boy called Mike Smithers leapt into the air in front of the goal and tried to head the ball into the net.

As he did so, the ball disappeared. In mid-air, it simply vanished from sight and, at the same time, there was a 'thunk' sound as Mike's head connected with something very solid and he collapsed to the ground.

The games master blew his whistle and came running over, and the rest of the players gathered around Mike as he lay groaning on the ground.

Tom and Geoff stared thoughtfully at the scene.

'Isn't there a map of the school grounds on a noticeboard by the main entrance?' Tom said eventually.

Geoff said he thought that there was.

'Only, if we can find out how far it's gone since this morning –' Tom studied the distance from the domestic science block to where they were putting Mike's body on a stretcher – 'we might be able to work out how long it would be before it got to the trees.'

Geoff looked doubtful. 'You mean . . . like maths?'

'Yes.' Tom wasn't entirely confident about the idea either, but it had to be worth a try.

They stood at the map in the main hall, and Tom measured the distances, while Geoff carefully wrote them down. According to the measurements, it was thirty-four centimetres from the fire escape to the front of the goalpost where Mike Smithers had bumped his head on Aquila, and a further thirty-seven centimetres from there to the other side of the field.

They had left Aquila at a quarter to nine that morning, and they knew it had been outside the goalposts at a quarter to one. All they had to do now was use this information to work out how fast it was going and how long it would be before it would get to the other side. It was a simple problem of arithmetic.

'What we need', said Geoff, thirty minutes later, 'is someone who knows about maths.'

'I'd never have believed it.' Mr Duncan was in the staffroom, addressing anyone who would listen. 'If I hadn't seen it with my own eyes, I swear I would never have believed it.'

'Baxter and Reynolds?' Miss Taylor had only come in on the tail-end of his story. 'Are you quite sure?'

'Positive,' Mr Duncan insisted. 'I found them in the form room, and there's no question. They were doing maths.'

'What sort of maths?'

'They were trying to work out a problem. I don't know where they got it from. Something about if A travels X centimetres in Y hours, how long is it before it gets to Z. Seriously! I couldn't believe it!'

'Was this homework or something?' asked Miss Poulson.

'No.' Mr Duncan shook his head. 'I haven't set any this week. It had nothing to do with their class-work.'

'So why were they doing it?'

'Fun,' said Mr Duncan. 'That's what they told me. Fun.' He shook his head in disbelief. 'And when I offered to explain what they were doing wrong, their little faces lit up. They were interested. They were hanging on every word like they really wanted to know . . . and then when I told them the answer – I forget what it was, four hours and something – they were so grateful. Extraordinary, isn't it? I really hadn't thought they were the type!'

Miss Taylor went back to her office wondering if the world had gone quietly mad. Baxter and

Reynolds doing maths . . .

That lunchtime she had already had to deal with a vanishing football, a concussed football player who had hit his head on thin air, and then, when she had tried to ring Mrs Baxter, an answerphone message said she had gone out.

And the one thing everyone knew about Mrs Baxter was that she never went out . . .

Aquila arrived at exactly the time Mr Duncan said it would.

At five minutes past five, there had been a creaking sound from the tree above them, and both boys had looked up to see one of the branches being slowly pushed aside by some powerful but invisible force.

Geoff had quickly swung himself up into the tree, pulled himself out along the branch and then vanished inside Aquila. A moment later he had flown down so that Tom could climb in beside him.

The first thing Geoff did when they were airborne was use the point from a pair of dividers to poke out the bit of chewing gum that had stuck in the forward control. Tom sat beside him, hungrily eating his lunch. His egg sandwiches had been badly flattened by the football, but he ate them anyway. It had been a long time since breakfast.

As they flew home, the boys were relieved to find that Aquila seemed none the worse for the experience. Nothing had changed, apart that is from a little purple light in the centre panel of the dash that had started flashing. Tom wondered if it meant something was wrong but, as Geoff pointed out, a flashing light can mean anything.

'My dad's got a light that flashes on his watch on his wedding anniversary,' he said. 'It doesn't have to mean anything. It'll probably turn itself off after a while.'

But an hour later, as Tom sat in Aquila back in the garage writing up the day's events in his exercise book, he couldn't help noticing that the light was still flashing.

CHAPTER SEVEN

The noise began soon after six the next morning, though you could hardly call it just a noise. It was a high-pitched wailing, ululating sound, with a penetrating quality that woke Tom from a deep sleep and sat him bolt upright in bed.

He looked briefly at his clock before staggering to the window to see what was going on. The noise, he realized, was coming from the garage, and without even bothering to put on his slippers, he ran downstairs and out of the back door.

Outside, the noise was even louder and in the garage it was almost deafening. It came from Aquila, and it was accompanied by a pulsating purple glow that came from the light on the centre of the dashboard. Only now there was not one flashing light, but two.

For several seconds Tom stood there, wondering what to do. He knew that if the noise went on much longer, he would not be the only one coming to find out what was causing it. The only idea he could think of was to get in Aquila and fly it somewhere where the noise would attract less attention, but as he put a hand on the side to swing himself into the seat, the sound ceased.

The purple lights were still flashing, but the garage was completely silent. Tom took his hand off Aquila and stepped back, but the noise did not return. He was still trying to work out what it all meant when he heard his mother calling.

'Tom? What's going on?'

Tom emerged from the garage to find his mother standing on the step outside the back door.

'What on earth was all that noise about?' she asked.

'I don't know,' said Tom. 'I was wondering myself.'

'It sounded very close.' Mrs Baxter looked nervously around her for a moment, then stepped back into the kitchen. 'I suppose it was some sort of alarm.'

Tom followed his mother into the house.

'An alarm?'

'I don't see what else it could have been,' said Mrs Baxter. 'Do you?'

'If it *was* an alarm', said Tom, when Geoff came round and he told him what had happened, 'then it must mean something's wrong.'

'It doesn't look as if anything's wrong.'

Geoff sat in Aquila as it hovered, solidly, half a metre or so above the ground in Tom's garage. Apart from the flashing purple lights, there didn't seem to be anything different about it at all.

Geoff was in fact less worried about Aquila making a noise than the news that Tom's mother had actually come out to investigate. The decision to keep Aquila in Tom's garage had been based on the knowledge that Mrs Baxter never left the house. If she was going to start behaving normally, they would need to find somewhere else.

'She's not getting cured or anything, is she?' he asked.

'I think she's trying.' His mother had not said anything about it, but Tom had noticed a pair of outdoor shoes by the door when he came home the previous evening. He pointed to the lights again. 'I was wondering if they meant that something wasn't working right.'

'There's only one way to find out.' Geoff put his hands on the controls. 'Are you going to do the doors?'

Tom opened the garage doors and Geoff floated carefully outside, where he waited until his friend climbed in beside him. Keeping Aquila close to the ground, he flew slowly round the back of the house and into the garden.

Everything seemed to move just as it should. Aquila went to the right and the left, up and down, and swung from side to side as it had always done. There didn't seem to be anything wrong with it at all.

'All seems fine to me,' said Geoff, as he banked in a sweeping curve that took them somewhere over Mrs Murphy's rose garden.

'What was that?'

'What?'

Tom peered round. 'I heard a noise. A sort of knocking sound.'

'I didn't hear anything.' Geoff looked at his watch. 'Come on, we'll be late for school.' He swung Aquila up and over the houses. 'Don't worry, I'll keep us low, just in case.'

Neither of them noticed Mrs Murphy standing in her rose garden. Several times in the last few days she had heard voices when there was no one there, and this time, when she had reached up, she had actually been able to touch and then knock on something solid in the empty air above her.

The doctor had advised her to get out and about more. Maybe he was right. He had also said that in an emergency she could take two of the new pills. As she tottered back to the house, she decided this was definitely an emergency.

'Come in!' Miss Taylor was in her office, lunching off a couple of pork pies, and she motioned Mr Urquart to a chair. 'You've heard about the maths?'

'Maths?' Mr Urquart looked blank.

'Peter Duncan found them yesterday in a class-room, doing arithmetic for fun.' Miss Taylor shook her head. 'This thing is getting stranger by the day.'

'Well, it's partly about the boys I wanted to see you.' Mr Urquart took a piece of paper from his briefcase. 'Tom anyway. I gave their class a test in geography this morning, and I thought you might like to see what he did.'

He passed the paper to Miss Taylor who stared at it, a section of pork pie frozen in mid-bite.

'I called it a general knowledge test', Mr Urquart explained, 'to see how much they knew about geology. The first ten questions were about recognizing types of rock – some of the bright ones scored a few marks there – and then I gave them ten more questions on putting geological ages in the right order. Nobody got any of those, except Tom.'

Miss Taylor looked at the row of ticks down the page and then at the total at the bottom. Twenty out of twenty. To her certain knowledge, Tom had never come top in anything before. There were thirty-six in his form, and the highest position he had ever reached was equal thirty-fifth.

'What I don't understand', said Mr Urquart, 'is why he never produces anything like this in any of his other work. You don't think he's been deliberately hiding his intelligence?'

'I know he's hiding something,' said Miss Taylor. 'I certainly never thought it might be intelligence.'

★

Tom was sitting with Geoff in Aquila outside the sweetshop between a couple of parked cars. Geoff had bought two ice creams and they were quietly eating, when a man walking along the pavement stopped in front of them and gave both boys a cheery smile.

'My word, what's this then?'

Tom and Geoff stared up at him.

The man bent and tapped Aquila's hull. 'Now that's the sort of vehicle I'd like. What is it?' He was looking directly at Tom.

'It's . . . It's . . .' Tom's mind froze. 'It's Geoff's,' he said eventually, pointing to his friend.

'Oh, yes?' The man looked brightly at Geoff. 'Where'd you get it from?'

'We got it from a man', said Geoff, slowly, 'who didn't want it any more.'

'I see. Left over from a film set, was it? Something like that?'

Neither of the boys replied.

'Well, I think you're very lucky. Wish I'd had one when I was your age.' The man looked at the dash. 'Flashing lights and everything, eh?'

He smiled again, and disappeared round the corner into the shop.

The boys looked at each other and then at the dashboard.

'I thought we were supposed to be invisible,' said Tom.

'We were when I got in.' Geoff was already climbing out to stand on the pavement. Both Aquila and

76

Tom, he saw, were in full view.

'I don't understand it.' He checked briefly that no one was in sight. 'Press the button again.'

As Tom pressed the button, Aquila disappeared, but the moment he took his finger away it came back again. Eventually, they used a piece of sticking plaster from the first-aid kit Mrs Baxter put in Tom's school bag to tape over the switch and keep it on. It worked but it was, as even Geoff admitted, a little disturbing.

'Flashing lights, engine knock, and a dodgy invisibility button,' he said. 'Doesn't sound too healthy. What we need is a proper test flight. I'm going to do some safety checks.'

'Safety checks?'

'I'll take it out somewhere and put it through its paces, you know? A few tight loops, hard turns, full throttle and plenty of speed changes. Then we'll see what breaks down.'

Tom had a feeling this might not be the way the professionals would conduct a safety check, but Geoff was very insistent.

'If anything else is going to go wrong,' he said, seriously, 'I think we need to know about it.'

Tom did not argue. He had just noticed a change to the flashing lights on the centre of the dash.

There were three of them now.

'What did his mother have to say?' asked Mr Urquart. 'Did you get a chance to talk to her?'

'I did.' Miss Taylor nodded. 'She came in to see me this morning.'

'She came in? What . . . into the school?'

'Yes . . .' Miss Taylor hesitated. It had not been an easy interview. Mrs Baxter, white and shaking, had gripped the sides of her chair and tried desperately to concentrate on answering the questions put to her, but when she had passed out for the third time, Miss Taylor had given up, carried her down to the car, and driven her home.

'You have to hand it to the woman,' she said. 'She was very determined. But hopefully I've persuaded her you need expert help to face these things. The doctor said he'd line her up with someone.'

'So she didn't say anything about Tom?' asked Mr Urquart.

'She said he likes rocks.' Miss Taylor glanced down at the test paper again. 'But we already know that, don't we?'

She had the distinct feeling that somewhere she had missed something. An important clue.

'Maybe we're going after the wrong person. Whatever they're doing, Geoff will be the one behind it, not Tom. He's the one we need to investigate.' Miss Taylor finished the last of her pork pie. 'I think I'll stop off at the newsagents on my way home. See what his father thinks . . .'

They took Aquila to the park in the end. If anything did go wrong, Geoff argued, and they crashed, they would do much less damage on grass or the lake than if they were flying over houses and streets. It was not a thought that Tom found particularly consoling.

Geoff flew three tight circuits. He began by hurtling over the water of the lake at a terrifying speed, then shot up through the trees, over the brow of the hill, down the other side, through the subway tunnel and a tight spin round to the main gates where they started. It was an exhilarating trip and, as Tom pointed out at the end, you couldn't say anything was wrong at all.

Geoff, however, was clearly not satisfied. 'I was on full speed that last bit.'

'Yes.' Tom was still trying to catch his breath. 'Yes, it felt like that.'

'No, you don't understand.' Geoff frowned. 'You remember how fast we went the first time I pressed the button?'

Tom remembered when they had shot out of the cave. It had taken them under a second to go half a mile. They had been travelling fast round the park, but not that fast.

'You had the button full on?' he asked.

'All the time.' Geoff paused for a moment. 'I think I know what the flashing lights mean.'

'What?'

'They're to warn us we're running out of power.'

'Like the light on a car that says you're running out of petrol?'

'Right.' Geoff pointed at the sticking plaster taped over the invisibility button. 'It would explain that as well. It's trying to cut out anything that uses too much energy.'

For a moment neither of the boys said anything, and then Tom broke the silence. It was a fairly obvious idea, but he thought it might be worth mentioning.

'Maybe we need to put in more petrol.'

Geoff looked at him.

'Well, I know it wouldn't be petrol,' said Tom. 'It'd be something else, but if we found what it was, we could maybe get some and put it in.'

'Like what?' said Geoff. 'I mean, what powers a machine like this?'

'I don't know.' Tom shrugged. 'But I suppose we could ask.'

CHAPTER EIGHT

Mr Bampford, the physics teacher, was a short, balding man who usually enjoyed answering children's questions, but preferred not to do it at the end of the school day, when he was trying to get back to the staffroom and smoke his pipe.

However, when Geoff and Tom appeared in front of him, holding out a copy of the *Sunday Mirror*, he stopped to listen. As far as he could remember, neither of the boys had ever spoken to him before, and he was curious to hear what they wanted to say.

'We were wondering what a UFO like this would have worked on,' said Geoff.

Mr Bampford took the paper and looked at the photograph on the front page.

'Worked on?'

'What it would have had in it,' said Geoff. 'You know . . . to make it go.'

'We thought possibly uranium,' put in Tom. 'Or plutonium?'

Mr Bampford studied the blurred image of Aquila for a moment before handing it back to Geoff. 'Apart from the fact that this photograph is an obvious fake –' he set off down the corridor towards the staffroom – 'I think any scientist would tell you that if there were such things as flying saucers, they would hardly be likely to run on anything as dangerous as radioactive isotopes.' He took his pipe out of his pocket as he walked. 'An advanced star-travelling technology would be capable of extracting the energy from more basic forms of matter.'

'Like what?' asked Geoff.

'Anything.' Mr Bampford took out a box of matches. 'Did you know that theoretically there's enough energy in a sugar lump to supply a city the size of New York with electricity for a week?'

'You're saying it runs on sugar lumps?' said Geoff.

'I'm saying that if your technology is advanced enough, you could run something like that on any form of matter you chose.' Mr Bampford stopped as he reached the staffroom door. 'Even the molecules from something as simple and basic as sugar.'

'You mean it could run on anything?'

'Anything at all.' Mr Bampford pushed open the door. 'Now, if you'll excuse me, I have an important staff meeting to attend.'

It had been a disappointing conversation, Tom thought, as he and Geoff walked back to the domestic science block. If Aquila could be powered by anything, then their chances of finding out what it was, were slim to say the least.

Not that it made much difference, he thought. Even if Mr Bampford had told them exactly what Aquila needed, they would still have had the problem of finding where to put it. Aquila's hull had no visible openings that they had ever found. Not so much as a glove compartment.

'I've been thinking about that,' Geoff said when Tom told him. He paused with one foot on the bottom rung of the fire escape. 'And maybe that's what we need to know first. Not *what* the fuel is, but where it goes.' He started up the ladder. 'I mean, if we found where the fuel tank was, and it had a bit of fuel left in it, we could look at what was in there, find out what it is, and maybe get some more of it.'

There was, Tom admitted, a certain logic to this.

'Like, if we found the end of a sugar lump, we could go out and buy some more sugar?'

'Exactly.' Geoff clambered off the ladder and disappeared into Aquila. Tom followed him.

'But we don't know where the fuel tank is, do we?'

Geoff settled himself at the controls, and gestured to the row of lights in front of them.

'No. But I should imagine it's opened by one of these.'

The plan Geoff outlined was very simple. They would press each of the lights in turn, starting at the top and working their way along the rows from left to right, and each time they pressed a button, they would check to see if any secret doors or flaps opened up on Aquila.

Both boys were acutely aware that the last time they had pressed a button, they had started eleven fires, but Geoff suggested that if they took Aquila to some isolated part of countryside, they would at least be unlikely to actually kill anyone.

Then they discovered that Aquila would never make it to the open fields. As Geoff flew Aquila away from the side of the domestic science block, he found Aquila's top speed had slowed to little more than a walking pace, and Tom pointed out that there were now four of the purple lights flashing from the dash.

Instead, they went to the park. It had a hill at one end, the remains of an iron-age fort, with a hollow in the top that they hoped would not only conceal them from passers-by, but also prevent them doing too much damage if they found anything like the laser beam again.

The first three buttons Geoff tried produced some interesting results, but none of them seemed to have anything to do with fuel. The first changed the colour of the underside of Aquila to a deep blue – for what reason, they never discovered. The second heated the seats, unfortunately to a degree that was a shade more than comfortable, and the third pro-duced a hologram in the air directly in front of them consisting of two words.

'*SERVUS STO.*'

The boys had no idea what either of them meant.

The results of pressing the fourth button, however, were rather more dramatic.

It started with a loud humming sound and then a thread of blue light appeared from under Aquila. It was not a straight beam, as the laser had been, but more like a moving coil that undulated over the grass in front of them, writhing like a snake and rapidly extending in length as if reaching out for something.

Tom found it slightly unnerving and wanted to turn it off, but Geoff was not so sure.

'It could be a fuel line,' he said hopefully, as the blue light twisted its way up to the lip of the hollow. 'Maybe it's looking for fuel. And when it finds some it'll bring it back.'

If Tom thought this was unlikely, he also realized that it was no more unlikely than most of the things that had happened since they found Aquila. The truth was that neither of them had ever had much idea what they were doing.

Until it was too late.

Reynolds' Newsagents stood at the end of a row of four shops, serving a housing estate that had been built on the east side of Stavely in the seventies. When Miss Taylor walked in, both Mr and Mrs Reynolds were serving behind the counter, and the shop was busy with customers.

Mr Reynolds, a large, confident, good-looking

man, gave her a cheery wave as soon as he saw her and, ignoring everyone in the queue, came over to ask how he could help.

'I wanted a word about Geoff, if you had a moment,' said Miss Taylor. 'But don't worry if you're busy. I'm quite happy to wait.'

'Wouldn't hear of it.' Mr Reynolds led Miss Taylor to a door at the back of the shop. 'Can't keep a busy woman like you waiting, Miss Taylor. You come on through.'

Experience had taught him that it was not wise to leave Miss Taylor in the shop for any length of time. In the course of her career, she had taught a good many of his customers and she had a habit, if given the chance, of telling them not to waste their money on chocolate and reminding them how unhealthy it was to buy cigarettes.

He ushered her straight through to the sitting room and pulled up a chair. 'So what trouble's he in this time then? Nothing too serious, I hope?'

'It's not really trouble at all,' said Miss Taylor. 'It's just his behaviour recently has been a little . . . odd.'

'Odd?'

'Yes.' Miss Taylor hesitated. It was not easy to put what she felt into words. 'He's been seen in the library a couple of times, and he's been asking questions in class, wanting to know about things . . .'

'Asking questions?' Mr Reynolds' face furrowed with concern. 'Right. I'll have a word with him about that.'

'No, no, we don't mind,' said Miss Taylor. 'In fact it's the sort of thing we encourage. It's just that Geoff's never done it before. It seems to have started on this geography field trip he went on. You haven't noticed anything different about his behaviour since then?'

Mr Reynolds thought for a moment, then shook his head.

'There's nothing he's done?' Miss Taylor persisted. 'Nothing he's said or talked about?'

Mr Reynolds dug deep in his mind to try and remember anything that Geoff might have talked about in the last week. 'I could ask Mrs Reynolds,' he said eventually. 'I know she listens to the lad sometimes.'

Mrs Murphy was walking home through the park, her shopping trolley loaded with cat food. As she paused to catch her breath at the point where the path circled the crest of the old fort, the sound of a low humming caused her to look up.

The noise grew louder, and a moment later a cord of blue light appeared over the edge of the hill, paused for a second, as if it were an animal sniffing the air, and then turned towards Mrs Murphy.

Mrs Murphy backed away, but the light was already moving straight towards her, purposefully humming its way down the side of the hill, gathering speed as it did so. In rising panic, Mrs Murphy began to run. She moved with remarkable speed for an eighty-three-year-old with bad legs, but she was no match for the light. In a last desperate effort to get away, she abandoned her trolley and then watched in horror as a second later, the blue light caught it, engulfed it, and began dragging it back up the hill.

'My shopping!' Mrs Murphy called to anyone who could hear. 'Help! It's taken my shopping! And my purse. It's stolen my purse!'

Sitting in Aquila, Geoff and Tom could not hear Mrs Murphy's cries, but they watched in fascination as the tip of the blue light reappeared over the brow of the hill, pulling something along with it.

'Wow . . . what is that?'

'I'm not sure,' said Tom. 'But it looks like a shopping trolley.'

Geoff reached out and turned off the button. The light disappeared and the trolley fell over sideways on the grass. In the silence, they could hear Mrs Murphy calling for help, and then a man's voice asking what had happened.

'We'd better get out of here,' said Tom.

'Right.' Geoff pulled the sticky tape over the invisibility button, and put his hands on the controls. There were several voices now, and they were getting nearer.

'Geoff?' Tom wondered what his friend was waiting for. 'I think we should go home. I think we should go home now.'

'We can't.' A bead of perspiration trickled down Geoff's face.

'What?'

'We can't.' His thumb was pressing the up button as hard as he could. 'This is it. Full speed.' He stood up briefly, and then sat down again. 'And we're not invisible either.'

As Tom slowly absorbed this information, both boys could hear the voices drawing closer. Several people were scrambling up the other side of the slope and in a few seconds' time, the men looking for Mrs Murphy's shopping trolley would come over the hill. They would see the boys and Aquila. They would ask questions. They would want to know . . .

It was finished. The whole adventure was over, and they both knew there was nothing they could do about it. Geoff's hands fell from the controls and they waited.

It was all they could do.

As if to express how they felt, it suddenly started to rain.

Miss Taylor's conversation had not been as productive as she had hoped. According to Mrs Reynolds, her son had no new interests, hobbies or friends, and was behaving in exactly the way he had always done. He did go out a bit more these days, she admitted, but she had no idea where he went.

'I'm sorry he's causing you all this bother,' Mr Reynolds said as Miss Taylor finally stood up to leave. 'But I'll have a word with him. Make sure he keeps out of the library, that sort of thing.'

'Please don't.' Miss Taylor sometimes wondered if Geoff's father had fully grasped what children going to school was really about. 'In fact, I'd rather you didn't mention that I'd been here at all, if that's all right?'

'Anything you say,' said Mr Reynolds, cheerfully.

As he led Miss Taylor back out to her car, he suddenly remembered something.

'There is one thing he's got interested in.'

'Yes?'

'Just this last week, too.' Mr Reynolds couldn't imagine why he had not thought of it before. 'UFOs. He's got interested in flying saucers. He likes me to check in the morning. See if there's anything about them in the papers.' Mr Reynolds smiled happily. 'There. I knew there was something.'

'Thank you,' said Miss Taylor.

It wasn't the sort of information she had expected, but she filed it carefully away in her mind as she put the car into gear and drove off. It might only be a small piece of the jigsaw, but experience had taught her that was always how you arrived at the final picture.

One piece at a time.

It was Tom who noticed it first.

It was raining quite hard – one of those sudden heavy showers that can soak you to the skin before you even have time to open the umbrella – but neither of them was getting wet.

Nor was Aquila. As Tom looked, he could see the raindrops splashing down towards the hull, but somehow without ever seeming to connect. Aquila's surface remained perfectly dry, as if the rain was being absorbed before it could land.

A man's face appeared over the brow of the hill. It was an elderly figure with a walking stick, which he pointed down the slope.

'There it is!' He started walking towards the shopping trolley on its side on the grass.

Another man – a park attendant – scrabbled up the slope to join him.

'I'll get it. You wait here.' He had his coat pulled over his head to keep off the rain and he climbed down towards the trolley as two more men appeared, half carrying, half dragging a rather bedraggled Mrs Murphy.

'This your trolley, missus?' asked the park attendant, as he pulled it upright. Mrs Murphy nodded.

'Why aren't they looking at us?' said Geoff. 'Why haven't they said anything?'

'I don't think they can see us.' Tom was still looking at the water not landing on Aquila. He had suddenly remembered what Mr Bampford had said about an advanced technology being able to extract energy from almost anything.

He pointed to the purple lights at the centre of the

dash. Only two of them were flashing now and, as he watched, one of those blinked into stillness.

'Water.' Tom could hardly believe it, even as he said it. 'It runs on water.'

That evening in the garage, Tom filled Aquila from a garden hose. It was a strange sight. The water cascaded on to Aquila's hull and . . . disappeared. For almost two hours he ran the tap at full flow, and for almost two hours the water vanished somewhere into Aquila, before suddenly splashing off the surface and on to the floor, and Tom hurriedly went to turn off the tap.

As the water was running, Tom tried to calculate how much of it Aquila was taking on. He knew the hose could fill a two-gallon watering can in about half a minute, so in two hours Aquila must have absorbed . . . quite a lot. He thought it might be worth working out exactly how much, as it seemed to be more than there was physically room for it to hold. Which would be interesting.

Geoff left Tom to look after the water. Sitting in Aquila, he pressed the third button from the left on the top, and watched as the hologram of words appeared in the air in front of him.

'*SERVUS STO.*'

Laboriously he set about copying the words, one letter at a time, on to a piece of paper. He had a strong desire to find out what they meant.

CHAPTER NINE

Mr Urquart looked at the bit of paper and then at Geoff.

'Where did you find this?'

'We saw it written down somewhere.'

'And you want to know what it means?'

'I tried looking the words up,' Tom put in, helpfully, 'but they weren't in the dictionary.'

'I'm not surprised.' Mr Urquart stared at the bit of paper again. 'It's in Latin.'

'Latin?'

Geoff tried to sound as if this were of only casual interest.

'Which wasn't my best subject,' Mr Urquart continued, 'though I did scrape a GCSE.' He handed the paper back to Geoff. 'How can I help you?'

'Well . . . we want to find out what it means.'

'That *is* what it means.' The bell rang for the start of lessons, and Mr Urquart sat down at his desk.

'Roughly speaking. A literal translation would be "I stand ready to serve". Now, unless there's anything else?'

'No. Thank you.'

Geoff and Tom walked to their seats at the back of the class. It was better than either of them had dared hoped. If a machine asks how it can help you, then it is probably expecting you to ask for some sort of help. And there were plenty of ways the boys could think of that Aquila might be able to do that.

Unfortunately, it had asked them in Latin, presumably a consequence of the fact that it had belonged to a Roman, so conversation was not going to be easy.

'Try the library at lunchtime, shall we?' Geoff murmured as they sat down.

'Good idea,' said Tom.

They found seven books on Latin in the library. They were ink-stained and shabby, and dated from the days when learning Latin at school had been as commonplace as doing Maths or English. There were three dictionaries, two grammars, a copy of *Caesar's Gallic Wars* and a paperback called *Latin Made Simple*, written for people who were trying to teach themselves.

Tom started with the dictionaries.

Geoff's idea was that they should make up a simple question in Latin to ask Aquila. It didn't matter what the question was, he said, all they needed was something they could try out. If Aquila answered the question, even if it was an answer the boys could not understand, they would at least know they were on the right track.

But it was turning out to be a more difficult task than they thought. Geoff had suggested translating something short like 'What does this light do?' or 'How high can you go?', but even such simple sentences were not easy to translate. The dictionary, for instance, did not have anything for the word 'does', but had a choice of nine different words for 'can'. Looking at the grammar books was no help at all. They were filled with pages of details about irregular deponent verbs of the fourth conjugation that meant nothing to the boys at all.

'Typical, isn't it,' muttered Geoff.

'What?'

'The one subject that might actually be useful, and schools don't teach it any more.'

Tom was flipping through the pages of *Latin Made Simple*.

'If it doesn't matter what we ask, I suppose we could try one of these.' He pointed to one of the exercises set at the end of a chapter. It was a series of sentences to be turned into Latin, and one or two of them were questions.

'I know they're in English here,' said Tom, 'but it's got the answers at the back of the book.'

'What sort of questions?' asked Geoff.

'Are they in the garden with the boys?' Tom read.

It wasn't exactly the sort of thing you were burning to know, Geoff thought, but it might serve their purpose.

The news was greeted in the staffroom with understandable disbelief.

'They're what?' asked Miss Taylor.

'They're teaching themselves Latin.' Miss Poulson couldn't help smiling as she said it. 'Graham Urquart found them in the library.'

'Reynolds and Baxter? Learning Latin?' Miss Taylor stared at her across the coffee table. 'Are you serious?'

'I know it's odd.' Miss Poulson had just come from the library. 'But that's what they were doing.'

'It's not odd. It's unbelievable.' Miss Taylor frowned. 'What did Graham say exactly?'

'Just that he found them at one of the tables surrounded by dictionaries, notepads and paper, beavering away . . .'

'Oh, this is ridiculous!' Miss Taylor snorted. 'Those two boys are doing something, and I demand to know what it is!'

Geoff pressed the button.

'*SERVUS STO*' appeared in the air, just as before, and Tom read out the first of the questions he had highlighted in the book.

'*Suntne in horto cum pueris?*'

The reply was instantaneous, and was a single word.

'*NESCIO.*'

'It talks.' A beatific smile spread across Geoff's face. 'It talks!'

'Unfortunately, it only talks Latin.' Tom started carefully copying the word on to a piece of paper. 'I wonder what it means.'

'We can find out what it means.' Geoff leant back in Aquila with a smile of satisfaction. 'What matters is, it talks. Go on, ask it one of the others.'

Tom read the next question from the book.

'*Cur magistri puellas oppugnabant?*'

It meant 'Why were the masters attacking the girls?' and again, Aquila's reply was instantaneous.

'*QUAE PUELLAE?*'

'Oh, this is great!' Geoff smiled happily. 'This is fantastic. Give us another one, go on!'

When he had finished copying the reply, Tom asked the next question, and the result this time was a lot more than a couple of words. Whole pages of writing suddenly filled the air in front of them, arranged in a curved space around them that was over two metres long and about a metre high.

'Wow!' Geoff breathed. 'What did you ask that time?'

'Which country do you come from?' said Tom. He knew he would never be able to copy down all the reply, but he made a start on the first sentence.

'Neat. Really neat.' Geoff nodded happily. His

only worry was how long it might take Tom to translate all these replies. In the library, when they had asked Mr Urquart how long it took people to learn Latin, he had said eight or nine years was not uncommon.

Geoff did not want to wait that long.

What they needed was some expert help.

'Are you sure they weren't winding you up?'

'Quite sure.' In the library, Mr Urquart was showing Miss Taylor the table where the boys had been working. 'In fact I only found what they were doing by accident. They were trying to keep it a secret.'

'A secret?'

'They had a couple of football annuals propped up to hide what they were doing. If I hadn't come behind them to put some books away, I'd never have known.'

Miss Taylor shook her head. She still found the whole thing very difficult to believe. 'I'm calling a meeting for four o'clock this afternoon,' she said. 'I want anyone who teaches those boys or has even talked to them in the last fortnight to be there. We have to get to the bottom of this. Is that all right with you?'

'Of course.'

'And we'll need all the information we can get. I wonder when the last time was that anyone searched their desks.'

'Searched their . . .?' Mr Urquart looked rather

startled. 'Wouldn't that be an invasion of privacy?'

Miss Taylor gave him a pitying glance. 'You'd better come with me to the classroom and show me where they sit.' She led the way out of the library. 'You've really no idea what this Latin business was about?'

'None at all.' Mr Urquart followed the Deputy Headmistress down the corridor to the form room. 'It just seemed they wanted to learn. Tom even asked if I could give him lessons, but I told him I wouldn't be much use. I said they'd need someone like Mr Hodge.'

Mr Hodge had come to Stavely Boys' Grammar School thirty-five years before, to teach Latin and Greek. As the years passed, the demand for these subjects had declined, the grammar school had become a comprehensive, and Mr Hodge had had to adapt his teaching abilities to other areas.

At the moment, he taught something called Home Skills, which involved helping young people learn the things they would need to know when they had houses and families of their own. It was not a job that suited him. Mr Hodge had no family and his house was notoriously unhygienic.

He was due to retire in a year, and the Board of Governors prayed that no student would actually die in one of his 'Safety in the Home' lessons before then. It looked like being a close run thing.

When Tom and Geoff found him, he was setting

out some ironing boards and irons, ready to teach 5D the finer points of ironing a shirt. He had snagged his fingers twice and had a nasty burn on his forearm which he was running under the cold tap.

'What do you want?' he asked when he saw the boys. He had a nervous, hunted look, and regarded most children with some suspicion.

'If it's not too much trouble,' said Geoff, 'we wondered if you could tell us what this means.' He passed over the paper on which Tom had written the replies that Aquila had made.

Mr Hodge looked at the paper.

'I don't know.'

'I thought you used to teach Latin,' said Tom.

'I did.' Mr Hodge took his arm from under the cold tap and put on his glasses. 'That's what *nescio* means. First person singular of the verb not to know. The next one is "what girls?", and this last paragraph . . . is really rather interesting.' He looked up at the boys. 'Where did you get this?'

'It's a sort of puzzle,' said Geoff.

'Is it? It's not a text I've come across before, but it seems clear enough.' A curious change had come over Mr Hodge's face as he studied the words. The hunted look had disappeared, and his eyes glinted with enthusiasm. 'It says . . . "This life-raft was made by the people of Deneb in the fourth decade of the reign of the Emperor D'BengPar, as part of one of the many flying warships built to defend his property from the treacherous and deceitful Yrrillian."' He paused. 'Does that mean anything to you?'

'Where's Deneb?' asked Tom.

'I've no idea.' Mr Hodge shook his head. 'The only Deneb I've heard of is a star. Somewhere in the constellation of Cygnus. Would that fit your puzzle at all?'

'Yes.' Geoff nodded slowly. 'It might fit rather well.'

'It's beautifully phrased.' Mr Hodge read the Latin to himself once more, relishing the words as they rolled off his tongue, but before he could finish, the water in the sink overflowed on to the power cable leading to one of the irons. There was a loud bang as the fuse blew, and Mr Hodge stepped back in alarm. He tripped over the end of an ironing board, banged his head on the corner of a table, and fell to the floor.

Tom and Geoff waited with him till the ambulance arrived. It seemed the least they could do in return for his help, though they were both anxious to write down the translation he had given them before they forgot it.

As soon as she saw it, Miss Taylor knew that she had found what she was looking for.

The exercise book had been lying quite openly in Tom's desk. On the cover, was written 'Aquila' in large capital letters, and underneath it was a drawing of an eagle, carrying a banner in its mouth with the words '*Licet volare, si in tergo aquilae volat.*'

She flipped through the pages in which Tom had carefully recorded everything that had happened since the day Geoff had fallen into the cave. As well as the writing, there were maps, newspaper cuttings, and drawings of the dashboard of Aquila, with careful descriptions of what some of the lights did.

As Miss Taylor turned the pages, everything slotted into place. However unlikely, she knew there was only one explanation that could possibly fit all the facts.

She passed the book to Mr Urquart, who riffled through it, and gave a low whistle.

'We need a photocopy,' said Miss Taylor. 'And then we have to get this book back in his desk before afternoon lessons. I don't want them to suspect anything. Not yet.'

They finally had the answer they'd been looking for, Geoff realized. At the front of the class, Miss Poulson was talking about the Treaty of Versailles, but Geoff, in a world of his own, was not even pretending to listen.

Aquila could talk. They could ask it what each of the various buttons did. They could find out when it had been made, and who for. They could ask it what the matter was if anything went wrong. It could tell them what it could do, how it worked, who the Yrrillians were . . .

The answers, of course, would be in Latin, and they would not be able to ask Mr Hodge for translations on any regular basis, not without arousing suspicion, but Tom would get the hang of it eventually. Geoff had great faith in his friend. He was a lot smarter than most people realized.

Beside him, Tom was busily filling in the details of the day's events in the exercise book he had taken from his desk.

'It explains why there was nothing written down at the site, doesn't it?' he whispered.

'What?'

'I always wondered why the centurion didn't have anything written down. Like a book of instructions, to remind him what all the lights did.' Tom pointed to his exercise book. 'I mean, I've written everything down, but he didn't have to, did he? All he had to do was ask.'

Geoff looked at Tom's book. 'You've written everything down in there?'

'Yes.' Tom looked up. 'Why? What's wrong?'

'Nothing really,' said Geoff. 'Only I don't think you should leave it in your desk. We don't want anyone else to find it, do we?'

CHAPTER TEN

The start of Miss Taylor's meeting was delayed for some minutes by the late arrival of Mr Hodge who had been at the hospital having his head X-rayed, but at a quarter past four it finally got under way.

'I'd like to thank you all for giving up your time at such short notice.' The Deputy Headmistress looked round at the dozen or so members of staff seated in her office. 'As you've possibly heard, I'm concerned about the activities of two boys – Tom Baxter and Geoff Reynolds – who were found this morning, in the library, trying to teach themselves Latin.'

A murmur of shock and concern ran round those of the staff who had not yet heard about this.

'In the last four days,' Miss Taylor continued, 'these same boys have approached Derek Bampford to ask about advanced power technologies. They asked Amy Poulson about the early navigation techniques used in the Flying Corps, and Peter Duncan found them on Monday trying to solve a maths problem in their free time . . . for fun.'

'They were at it again this morning,' Mr Duncan chipped in. 'Came to me at the end of the lesson. Wanting to work out something about a tap, a watering can and how big was the bath it filled in two hours.'

'Thank you, Peter.' It was the first Miss Taylor had heard about that one. 'Now, that is exactly why we're here. I want to know what's going on, and the first thing we need to do is pool any information we have on their behaviour.' She looked around the room. 'Has anyone else noticed these boys doing anything odd in the last week or so?'

Eight people put their hands up.

At the controls of Aquila, Geoff banked to the right, and began a gentle descent that would carry them down towards Tom's garden. Both boys were filled with that deep satisfaction that comes from knowing that a difficult day has turned out rather better than either of them had dared to expect.

As Geoff said, once Tom had learnt to speak Latin, they would be able to ask Aquila so many things. They would be able to find out what the buttons did without the risks involved in just pushing them to see what happened. And when they knew what they did, they might even find out what some of them were for.

'Like that one,' said Tom, pointing to the button which had produced the blue light that had kidnapped Mrs Murphy's shopping trolley. 'I mean, what's it actually supposed to do?'

They were coming in over Mrs Murphy's garden as he said it and unfortunately Geoff chose exactly that moment to swing Aquila round towards Tom's garage.

The unexpected movement shifted Tom forward in his seat, and his finger made a momentary contact with the button at which he had been pointing. The contact lasted for only a fraction of a second before Tom snatched his hand away, but it was too late. The damage had already been done.

Aquila was now on full power, and the blue cord of light that appeared beneath it, instead of lazily snaking its way out, flashed to the ground like a bolt of lightning.

'What was that?' Tom asked, as Geoff took his hands off the controls to stare at the ground beneath them.

'I think', said Geoff, 'that was Mrs Murphy.'

Mrs Murphy, in her garden, had been bending down to pick up one of her cats, when the bolt of blue light had engulfed her.

Neither she nor the cat had moved since.

Geoff landed Aquila by the burnt-out shed at the bottom of the old lady's garden, and the boys climbed out.

'Mrs Murphy?' Tom ran towards her. 'Mrs Murphy, are you all right?'

But Mrs Murphy did not reply. She still had not moved and, as Tom got closer, he realized she was not breathing.

Both she and the cat appeared to be completely frozen. Even her clothes and the cat's fur had a solid, unwavering look as if they'd been soaked in starch, and when Geoff stretched out a hand and tapped the old woman on the arm, it made a metallic ringing sound.

He opened his mouth to speak and then closed it again.

It was one of those times when it was difficult to know what to say.

'I've killed them, haven't I?' said Tom.

'Well . . .' Geoff looked closely at Mrs Murphy's face. 'I know she's not moving . . .'

'She's not breathing either.'

'No,' Geoff conceded, 'but if she was dead, wouldn't she have fallen down or something? I mean, she *looks* perfectly all right. Just . . . not moving.'

Tom's shoulders sagged. 'We'd better go and tell the police or someone.' He turned back to Aquila. 'My mother is not going to like this, you know. She is not going to like this at all . . .'

'Hang on.' Geoff caught his friend's arm. 'There is one thing we could try first . . .'

★

Miss Taylor had been taking notes. Most of the things people were saying, she had already known, but some details were new, and had surprised even her.

Mr Urquart had given a list of the eight books the boys had taken out of the library in the last week, which included titles such as *A History of Rome* and *Great Palaces of Europe*. Mr Rivers, head of the Science department, reported that they had also taken two books from his subject library – on lasers.

Mrs Ross, the English teacher, described how, after a lesson, the two boys said they had been reading H. G. Wells's *Invisible Man* and had quizzed her at some length on how invisibility might actually work. And the oddest revelation in some ways had come from Mr Weigart, in charge of Design Technology, who said that, the day before, he had found the two boys in his craft room trying to make a sextant.

Mr Duncan, when someone had explained to him what a sextant was, voiced the bemused astonishment of everyone there.

'What are they doing? What on earth is going on?'

'I think I may have the answer to that.' Miss Taylor stood up and started passing round a set of photocopies, neatly stapled together. 'If you'd all like to have a look at this? It's a copy of something we found in Tom's desk at lunchtime.'

Mr Bampford looked at the top page of his photocopy.

'Does anyone know what the Latin bit means?'

'It means "Any man can fly",' Mr Hodge spoke slowly and carefully, '"if he rides on the back of an eagle."' He looked across at the Deputy Head-mistress. 'I'm surprised to find a child today knowing something like that.'

'You wait till you see the rest of it,' said Miss Taylor.

Doctor Warner was sitting in her tent when the phone rang. Deep in thought, the archaeologist was contemplating the object that had been dug up that morning from the earth directly beneath the body of the Roman centurion. It was, she knew, quite impos-sible. But impossible or not, it continued to sit where she had placed it, on the table in front of her.

It was a 100 per cent authentic, Red Indian tomahawk.

The noise of the phone slowly penetrated her brain, and she picked it up.

'Yes, of course I remember you, Tom,' she said. 'What can I do for you?' She paused. 'You want the Latin for what?'

'Whatever you did to that woman, please could you undo it now,' repeated Tom.

There was a silence.

'Is that too difficult?'

'No. It's not difficult,' said Doctor Warner. 'I'm just wondering why anyone would want to say it.'

'We're sort of talking to someone,' Tom

explained. 'Like on the Internet. But they only speak Latin. Please,' he added. 'You're the only person we can think of to ask.'

Doctor Warner stared at the ceiling of the tent for a few seconds. '*Quidquid illi mulieri fecisti, id facias infectum,*' she said eventually. 'Was there anything else?'

'Could you hang on a bit?'

In the background she could hear Tom repeating the sentence she had given him, and a moment later he was back on the line.

'It says "*Quae femina?*" What would that mean?'

'It means whoever you've got there wants to know which woman you're talking about,' said Doctor Warner. 'Are you boys in some sort of trouble?'

'No, no. No trouble. How can we say "The woman in the garden"?'

'I think before I do anything else,' said Doctor Warner, 'I really would like to know what's going on.'

'Could we explain some other time?' asked Tom. 'Only it's a bit urgent.'

'Who are you talking to? And why are they talking in Latin?'

'I don't know,' said Tom. 'They just are.'

'But they must know another language. Why don't you ask them to use it?'

'We can't,' said Tom. 'You see . . .' He broke off. 'How exactly would we do that?'

'What?'

'How could we tell it to speak English, for instance,' said Tom. 'In Latin.'

Doctor Warner sighed. 'Try "*Utere Brittanica lingua.*" '

'*Utere Brittanica lingua,*' Tom repeated, and Doctor Warner heard a sharp intake of breath, a whoop of triumph, and somewhere in the background there was Geoff's voice shouting, 'Fantastic! Oh, wow! That is unbelievable!'

'Tom? Tom, are you there? Is everything all right?'

'Couldn't be better, Doctor Warner.' Tom's voice had a quietly triumphant ring. 'And thank you. Thank you very much indeed.'

The phone went dead. On reflection, Doctor Warner decided it had been one of the oddest conversations she had ever had, and she wondered briefly if she should tell someone about it.

Instead, she put down the phone and picked up the tomahawk from the table. As she ran it through her fingers, all thoughts of anything else drifted out of her mind.

In her hands, she knew, she held the first conclusive proof that, about a thousand years before Columbus, the Romans had discovered America.

All was quiet in the Deputy Headmistress's office, as the staff studied the photocopied pages Miss Taylor had given them, reading in an absorbed silence.

Mrs Ross was the first to speak. 'You're sure this

is all genuine?' she asked. 'Tom Baxter wrote this himself?'

'Every word,' said Miss Taylor. 'I've seen the original.'

'It's unbelievable,' said Mr Duncan.

'I agree. It's quite unbelievable. But it's there.' Miss Taylor leant forward over her desk. 'Individually, I know, none of the things we've talked about mean anything very much, but taken together and particularly in the light of this –' she gestured to the copy of Tom's exercise book – 'I think there is only one conclusion we can come to.'

Around her, there was a slow, but distinct nodding of heads.

'The question is . . . what are we going to do about it?'

Sitting in Aquila, Tom and Geoff stared at the words hanging in the air in front of them.

'WHAT CAN I DO FOR YOU?'

'I think', said Geoff, 'we'd like for you to always use English from now on.'

'OK.'

'No more Latin,' said Tom.

'OK.'

'And the first thing we want to know –' Geoff pointed to Mrs Murphy – 'is what you did to her?'

'WHO?'

'Mrs Murphy.' Tom pointed more carefully to

where Mrs Murphy stood, frozen in the act of picking up her cat. 'The woman over there.'

'SUBJECT HELD IN TEMPORAL STASIS.'

'Temporal stasis . . .' Tom read it aloud. 'What's that?'

Words filled the air in front of him. There was something in the first sentence about a six-dimensional matrix created by molecular displacement and fractal transpositioning, but none of it was remotely comprehensible.

'It doesn't matter what it is,' said Geoff. 'We just want it undone.' He turned to Aquila. 'Whatever you did to Mrs Murphy this morning –'

'And the cat,' said Tom.

'Right . . . and the cat. Whatever it was, we want you to undo it now.'

'Please,' said Tom.

'OK.'

A whiplash of moving light appeared from beneath Aquila, though this time it was a mauvish purple instead of blue. Quicker than the eye could follow, it reached out to engulf both Mrs Murphy and the cat . . .

and blinked out.

The cat gave a brief yowl, jumped down and ran into the house. Mrs Murphy stood up looking rather puzzled, and swayed dangerously backwards. Tom jumped out of Aquila and ran over to catch her before she fell. Geoff brought up a garden chair so she could sit down.

'Are you all right?' asked Tom.

'I think so.' Mrs Murphy sounded rather out of breath. 'I don't know what happened, but . . . I was trying to pick up Percy, and . . . Oh, dear!' She held her head.

'Let's go indoors and get you a glass of water,' suggested Tom.

'Thank you.' Mrs Murphy smiled at him. 'How lucky I am you boys came round.' Hanging on to Tom's arm, she tottered into the house. 'I'm having a lot of trouble with these pills the doctor's given me. You know, I've a good mind to go back to being depressed. It seemed a lot less bother.'

The excitement of the day's discoveries made it difficult for Geoff to sleep that night.

Aquila was parked just outside his bedroom window, and at midnight, still wide awake, he gave up trying to sleep, got out of bed, and climbed outside to sit at the controls.

He did not want to go anywhere. He was content simply to sit there, six metres in the air, with the night sky around him, his face gently illuminated by the lights from the dash.

They could no longer leave Aquila in Tom's garage. Tom had got home that day to find Mrs Baxter busily clearing things out to make room for the car she said she intended to buy. Apparently her treatment was progressing far faster than anyone had expected.

Geoff had suggested that he keep Aquila outside his bedroom. It would be well off the ground so no one would walk into it, and in the morning, all he would have to do was step out of the window . . .

While he was sitting there, he would have liked to ask Aquila some of the questions he had about how old it was, why exactly it had been made, and what it could do, but without Tom to read the answers there was little point.

And then he realized that there was one question he had that did not require reading for an answer, and he pressed the small green light, third in from the left.

'WHAT CAN I DO FOR YOU?'

'I want to know how far you can go, without having to fill up with water again,' said Geoff. 'In miles.'

The number that stretched out in front of him began with a three, but consisted mostly of noughts. Row upon row, line upon line of them, metre upon metre.

Geoff smiled in satisfaction. It seemed you could go a very long way in Aquila.

At midnight, the lights in Miss Taylor's office were still burning as well. She had a spent a large part of the evening making phone calls to various authorities, explaining the situation, and how she thought it should be handled. Then there had been the paperwork to complete – the forms to fill in, the instructions for her staff, the timetable for action.

It was important to act quickly and decisively, she thought, before the boys knew what was happening and had time to react.

Carefully, she checked through her notes one last time.

CHAPTER ELEVEN

'I wonder why she wants to see us?' asked Tom. 'We haven't done anything wrong, have we?' He remembered the telegraph poles, the eleven fires and freezing Mrs Murphy, and added, 'Well, nothing she knows about.'

Geoff only grunted. He was less concerned with what the Deputy Headmistress might want than with what they should do about Aquila. Losing Tom's garage as a hiding place had turned out to be more serious than either of the boys had realized. Leaving Aquila outside his bedroom window last night had seemed a simple enough solution, but this morning Geoff had realized he would not be able to keep it there on any permanent basis.

It had rained that morning, and Mr Reynolds, who always took the dog out for a quick walk before opening the shop, had noticed something so peculiar as he came back, that he called Mrs Reynolds and Geoff out of the house to have a look.

'See that?' He pointed to a section of the paving that ran round the side of the house. 'It's all dry. Everywhere else is getting wet, but this bit stays dry.' He squinted up at the sky by Geoff's bedroom window. 'It's like there's something up there, stopping the rain coming down.'

Geoff had seized the first opportunity he could to move Aquila to the bottom of the garden, but he had found there were risks to leaving it there, as well. He had left it by a tree a few metres in the air so that the dog wouldn't bump into it, but when it was time to set off for school, he found falling leaves had settled on the invisible hull in a way that looked decidedly odd. If anyone had cared to look down the garden, they could not have helped but notice.

Aquila was safe at school, for the moment at least. They had been able to leave it in its usual place by the fire escape because the ground beneath was already wet, but as Geoff pointed out, what they really needed was a new hiding place. Preferably somewhere indoors, out of sight, where nobody else ever went. He was beginning to understand why the Roman centurion had kept Aquila in a cave.

'I think we should go looking at lunchtime,' he said as they walked down the corridor to Miss Taylor's office. 'You know, float around town a bit. See if we can find anywhere.' He straightened his tie and knocked at the door. 'After all, the last thing we want is to lose it now.'

The first shock for the boys as they entered the office was finding Geoff's parents and Tom's mother were already there waiting.

Miss Taylor was sitting behind her desk and in front of her to the right were Mr and Mrs Reynolds. Mrs Baxter was sitting to the left, and between them there were two chairs where Miss Taylor indicated the boys should sit down.

Behind the desk, Mr Urquart was sitting on one side of the Deputy Headmistress, and on the other sat Miss Stevenson. Her presence alone would have told the boys that this was no ordinary meeting.

Miss Stevenson was the Special Needs teacher. An ex-Olympic shot-putter, she was in charge of those children who, for whatever reason, could not be taught in normal classes. Miss Taylor liked to have her around on those occasions when she thought physical restraint might be necessary. Her mere size was a very powerful deterrent.

'Well . . .' Miss Taylor looked across at the boys as they sat down. 'It seems you two have had a rather busy week – and you've certainly managed to pull the wool over everyone's eyes, haven't you?'

Mrs Reynolds put her hand on Geoff's knee. 'Why didn't you tell us?'

'Tell you what?' said Geoff, but of course he already knew.

As if to confirm his fears, Miss Taylor picked up

the photocopy of Tom's exercise book from her desk, and held it up for the boys to see.

'We've been reading this rather interesting document,' she said. 'It is yours, isn't it, Tom?'

Tom could not speak, but he nodded.

'Though I imagine it was a combined effort.' Miss Taylor shifted her gaze to Geoff. 'It says here, for instance, that you were the one who worked out how to bring Aquila home, Geoff. Is that true?'

'Yes,' said Geoff.

'Quite a clever idea.' Miss Taylor sniffed. 'In fact there are several clever ideas in here. I rather admired the way you tackled finding out what the power source might be. You said you liked that one, didn't you, Miss Stevenson?'

'Yes, I did.' Miss Stevenson nodded vigorously. 'I thought it was an intelligent piece of thinking, for an eleven-year-old.'

'Intelligent . . .' Miss Taylor repeated slowly. 'Yes, that's a word that keeps cropping up.' She picked up a piece of paper from her desk. 'And we already know that Tom is intelligent. Intelligent enough to come top of the class in this test on knowledge of geology, for instance.'

Tom noted with one part of his mind that Miss Taylor was holding up his last geography test, but mostly he was wondering why she had not yet launched into a lecture on how irresponsible and dangerous their behaviour had been and how they should hand over Aquila, while she called the police.

'So, we have two boys –' Miss Taylor carefully pressed her fingers together – 'who have always come bottom of the class, who hardly ever produce any work, but both of whom are apparently quite intelligent. How would you explain that, Miss Stevenson?'

'Well, I've been looking through their records.' Miss Stevenson opened a file on the desk, and Geoff realized with a shock that she had all his school reports and work records dating back to his primary school. 'And although we've always known that Geoff was dyslexic, I think it's much more severe than anyone realized. He's been able to disguise the fact partly because he's clever, and partly because he's always had Tom to help him out.'

'I see.' Miss Taylor nodded. 'And what about Tom? He can read, so why does he always come bottom as well?'

'I think Tom is the cautious sort of boy, who doesn't like to be rushed.' Miss Stevenson seemed to have a file with all his reports as well. 'He doesn't like writing things down, mostly because he's worried about making mistakes. He did all right in that geography test because rocks are the one thing he doesn't just know about, he *knows* that he knows.'

'Yes . . .' Miss Taylor leant back in her chair. 'So, we have two intelligent boys, who are doing badly at school, but who we know from this highly imaginative piece of work –' she tapped the photocopy of Tom's book – 'are the sort of children who like to solve problems, to know things, to find things out. And my job is to decide what we need to do about it.'

A faint suspicion was growing in Tom's mind. It seemed almost impossible and yet . . .

'Because the one thing we do know', Miss Taylor continued, 'is that the present system is not working. At the moment, you're not learning anything at all. So my colleagues and I have worked out a new timetable, which I think you'll find gives you more of what you need.'

She picked up two timetable forms, and passed them to the boys. His mother, Tom noticed, already had one.

'We'll go through them in detail in just a moment, but first I'd like to point out that most of the lessons will be just the two of you with a single member of staff, and with a particular emphasis on the basic skills of reading and writing. This will also be true of the extra lessons –'

'Extra lessons?' Geoff had been staring at his timetable. 'You're giving us extra lessons?'

'That's the idea, yes.' Miss Taylor looked at Geoff. 'There's a great deal to catch up on, you know, and without the extra hours . . .'

'This is the punishment, is it?'

Miss Taylor frowned.

'It's not a punishment.' Mrs Reynolds turned to her son. 'It's to help you.'

Geoff stared at his mother and then at the Deputy

Headmistress, utterly baffled. Then he looked across to Tom, and the answer came to them both, like a thunderclap.

They didn't know!

Miss Taylor had it all written down in front of her . . . and she didn't know. None of them knew.

It was like the man who had found them outside the sweet shop. He had actually seen them sitting in Aquila, and had presumed that it was some sort of toy. Miss Taylor and the others had read everything Tom had written in the exercise book, but they all thought it was a story. It had never even occurred to them that what was described there might be real.

'I hope you realize Miss Taylor's gone to a lot of trouble to work all this out for you.' Mrs Baxter was talking to Tom. 'I think the least you two boys can do is say thank you.'

'Thank you,' said Tom, and Geoff joined in as well. 'Thank you, miss. Thanks very much.'

And even a hardened veteran teacher like Miss Taylor was touched by the note of heartfelt, genuine gratitude in their voices.

Tom and Geoff ate their sandwiches at lunchtime, sitting in Aquila, thirty metres in the air, alongside the top of the church tower. The parish church of St Mary's stood at one of the high points of the town, and its tower had the most wonderful view across Stavely, though at the moment neither of the boys was paying it any particular attention.

'I still can't get over it,' said Tom. 'I mean, we were *so* lucky!'

He was feeding bits of his sandwich to a dazed-looking pigeon on Aquila's hull. One of the hazards of flying something invisible was that occasionally birds bumped into you. Tom was hoping that the pigeon had only been stunned and that it would shortly recover.

Geoff was staring at the timetable that Miss Taylor had given him, a deep frown on his face. The relief he had felt at the realization that they had not, after all, lost Aquila, had been slowly replaced in the hours that followed by a numb realization that what he had lost was most of his free time.

According to the timetable, he and Tom would soon be having lessons at lunchtimes, after school, and even at weekends. And these would be real lessons. With only the two of them in the class, there would be no sitting at the back trying to look stupid and letting someone else answer all the questions. They would have to work.

'It might be all right.' Tom knew what his friend was thinking. 'You never know, it might even help.'

'Help?' Geoff had vivid memories of the last time someone had tried to give him extra lessons in reading. He had been seven, and the process had consisted mostly of long periods of angry shouting. It was not an experience he wanted to repeat.

'Well, I still think we've been very lucky,' said Tom. He watched as the pigeon staggered to its feet and started walking in little circles round the hull. 'I mean, we've still got Aquila.'

'But nowhere to keep it any more.' Geoff was not normally a gloomy boy, but the new timetable had got him badly unnerved. 'Not that it matters much. With all these lessons, we won't have to time to fly anywhere anyway.' He threw down the timetable in disgust. 'I vote we go back and tell them they've made a mistake. Tell them they've got it all wrong.'

'You think that'd make Miss Taylor change it all?'

'Maybe not Miss Taylor,' said Geoff. 'But if we talked to Mr Urquart . . .' He paused. 'Look, if I go will you come with me? I think it ought to be both of us.'

Tom did not reply. His pigeon had just walked off the edge of Aquila and was dropping to the ground like a stone.

'Tom? Look, I need your help on this one. Are you going to come with me?'

'Yes. Yes, of course.'

Tom smiled. To his relief, just before it hit the ground, the pigeon had started to fly.

It was gone five o'clock before the boys emerged from the library and their first session of supervised homework, but they found Mr Urquart still in his classroom, preparing a map of Portugal for the next day's lessons.

'Hi, how's it going?' he asked, cheerfully.

'Well, the thing is,' said Tom, 'we think there may have been a misunderstanding.'

'Oh?'

'You've got it all wrong,' said Geoff. 'Completely wrong.'

Mr Urquart put down his pen and looked at the boys. 'Wrong about what?'

'This extra work you're giving us. You seem to think it's what we wanted. And we don't,' said Geoff. 'We don't want it at all.'

'Ah . . .' Mr Urquart looked thoughtfully at the boys. 'But that's not quite what you've been saying, is it?'

'We haven't been saying anything,' said Geoff. 'We haven't said anything to anyone.'

'That's why we sit at the back of the class,' explained Tom. 'So we don't have to speak to people.'

'And we don't want to learn,' said Geoff. 'We're quite happy not learning anything.'

'Now that's not true, is it?' Mr Urquart leant back in his chair. 'I mean, in the last week, you have both asked to visit an archaeological dig, you've been taking all sorts of books out of the library, you've been doing maths, you've been teaching yourselves Latin . . . Now, why would you be doing all that, if you weren't the sort of boys who wanted to learn, eh?'

Geoff opened his mouth to reply . . . and then closed it again.

'We want it to go back to how it was,' he said, stubbornly. 'We never wanted things to change.'

'But things are always changing.' Mr Urquart pushed his chair back from the desk. 'Nothing stays the same. It can't. You take Tom here. It's obvious that one day he's going to be some sort of geologist, but he can't do that without passing exams, and he'll have to start working for them sometime.'

He looked at Geoff. 'And there's yourself. Your parents told us this morning that you were very keen on flying. If you're going to be pilot or anything it's going to be important to be able to read, isn't it? To study maps. To know where you're going. To be able to understand the flight plan.'

Geoff stared at him for several seconds, and it was Tom who eventually broke the silence.

'You . . . you think I could be a geologist?'

'I think you can both be whatever you want, if you put your minds to it.' Mr Urquart stood up and walked over to the window. 'Look, I'm not saying it's going to be easy, but there are only two things you need to succeed in almost anything. One is the determination to do it, and the other is the right sort of help. Take your mother.' Mr Urquart looked across at Tom. 'She's a very good example. She doesn't leave the house for three years, and then one day she makes a decision. She's had enough. So she goes to the people who know how to help and whoompf! Next thing we know she's coming into school every other day and talking about buying a car. It's the same as you had written on the front of your book. "A man can fly anywhere, if he rides on the back of an eagle."'

Tom frowned. 'You think that's what it meant?'

'It's a proverb,' said Mr Urquart. 'From one of Aesop's fables. You know the story?'

Tom shook his head.

'The birds were having a competition one day to see who could fly the highest. Of course, everyone thought the eagle would win because he was the strongest, and had the biggest wings, and sure enough, when they all flew up into the sky, the eagle flew faster and higher than anyone else. But then, just when he had gone as far as he could, the sparrow, who had been sitting on his back, took off and flew higher still.

'That's how you get to do what you want in life. You decide where you want to go, and you find yourself an eagle.' Mr Urquart turned and stared out of the window. 'Eagles come in many forms, but they all have one thing in common. They carry you to the places you couldn't get to on your own. Sometimes to places you never even thought possible.'

In the playground below he could see Miss Taylor striding off towards the car park. There was something in the way she walked, with her head darting from side to side, that reminded him for a moment of a large predatory bird.

'They don't always have feathers and wings,' he said. 'Some of them even look like schoolteachers.'

CHAPTER TWELVE

When Geoff emerged from Miss Stevenson's house, it was with a strange feeling of content. Partly it was knowing that his two-hour Saturday morning session with the Special Needs teacher was over and that the rest of the weekend was his to do with as he liked, but it was something deeper as well.

There was, when Geoff considered it, a lot to be content about. In the three weeks since the meeting with Miss Taylor, they had found somewhere safe to keep Aquila, they had flown it the length and breadth of the country, and that afternoon they were planning to take it on their first flight across the Atlantic. It was only going to be a test run, a quick trip to New York and home again, but Geoff was rather looking forward to it.

He walked to the end of the road and turned left along the path that would lead him up to the old water tower. It had proved a very satisfactory hiding place. Built at the start of the previous century to provide water for the rows of terraced houses being constructed at the bottom of the hill, it was about fifty metres high, made of brick, and had been derelict for nearly thirty years.

The door and windows at the bottom were boarded up and surrounded with barbed wire, but at the top the boys had found just what they wanted. They had been able to fly in – the windows had neither frames nor glass – to a room that was large, dry, out of sight from anyone on the ground, and totally inaccessible.

There was, of course, the problem of how the boys were to get up and down themselves. If they left Aquila at the top of the tower, they would still need to be able to get down to go home, and they would need to be able to get back up again when they wanted to retrieve it.

The solution had been surprisingly simple. Going through the lights on the dash, asking Aquila to explain what each of them was for, they had come across one described as the 'PRE-SET SPATIAL CO-ORDINATE REGISTER FOR AUTOMATIC RETURN'.

What it meant was that Aquila was able to fly on its own. It did not need to have anyone at the controls. It did not even matter if there was anyone inside. At the instructed speed, and in perfect safety, it could fly to whatever destination it had been given.

The Roman centurion had known about it. They had found several of his settings still in Aquila's memory, and it made Tom shudder to realize that if Geoff had pressed a different button that first day in the garage, they could have found themselves flying to a small town in central Bulgaria.

They had given Aquila instructions that would make it fly to the top of the tower and back to the ground again, on a pre-arranged signal. Aquila could recognize signals in several thousand languages and as many frequencies, but the boys had settled in the end on using a dog whistle. Pitched to a level beyond the human ear, they had decided it would attract less attention.

The feeling of contentment stayed with Geoff as the path narrowed and he climbed through the wood. At the top, standing at the base of the tower, he blew three short blasts and two long on the whistle he took from his pocket. A moment later, he reached down to his right, felt Aquila's hull beside him and climbed in.

Aquila was programmed to arrive, invisible, to the right of whoever had blown the whistle, so it was wise to be careful where you were standing. The machine was very literal, and Tom had once blown the whistle while he was standing next to a tree. The stump was still there, and the trunk lay at the bottom of the hill, where it had fallen. The two parts had been cleanly separated in a way that still puzzled the man from the council who had been called out to investigate.

Sitting in Aquila, Geoff asked, 'Is Tom up there?'

'YES.' The letters flashed up in front of him, and beside them was a small line drawing, like a cartoon, of a boy sitting at a desk.

'He's working?'

'HE IS DOING HIS HOMEWORK.'

There was another drawing of Tom writing in an exercise book.

Aquila often used pictures when answering Geoff's questions, and it always used the simplest, shortest words. He had explained to it, very early on, that his reading was limited and asked it to speak, rather than writing words in the air.

Aquila, unfortunately, could not oblige. It could communicate in most of the known languages of the galaxy, but its vocal generator had been destroyed by an Yrrillian photon blast 6,000 years before. The mechanism had been situated somewhere in the discoloured twisted fin at the back, that the boys had noticed the first day they had found it.

But if Aquila could not help Geoff by talking, it could and did make the words it used as easy as possible for him to read, and on occasion both boys had found this useful. The week before, when they had been asking about the function of some of the lights, one was described as the 'CHLORINE ATMOS-PHERIC REGENERATOR'.

When Tom had asked what would happen if they tried it, Aquila said, 'NEGATIVE SURVIVAL POTENTIAL INDICATED FOR PRESENT

LIFE FORM,' which meant very little to either of them, but when Geoff asked the same question, it said, 'NO, NO! AGH!' and produced a little picture of a man coughing and spluttering until he keeled over and died. Chlorine, it turned out, is a very poisonous gas. In a way, it had been rather reassuring.

Aquila could have flown back up to the top of the tower on a simple command, but Geoff preferred to do it himself. Taking the controls, he spiralled up the tower in a series of circles, stopped outside the window at the top, and carefully backed inside.

The place looked rather homely these days.

Over in the corner, Tom was sitting at a table listening to music from an aged radiogram while finishing off his maths homework. He looked up as Geoff turned off the invisibility.

'Nearly finished.' He pointed to a mug. 'I got you a drink ready. It just needs heating up.'

As Geoff climbed out of Aquila, he couldn't help thinking how much his friend had changed in the last few weeks. If you had seen him last Sunday, leaning casually out of Aquila somewhere over the Pyrenees, determinedly banging away at a lump of basalt with a hammer, you would not have recognized him. There was a decisiveness in the way he moved and spoke these days, and if you saw him with Mr Urquart, talking confidently about fossil finds or why there were different colours in limestone, it was hard to believe he was the same person.

Collecting his mug, Geoff carefully placed it

under the rear fin. Aquila could heat a mug of drinking chocolate with a controlled blast of microwaves in a fraction of a second. It was only one of many conveniences, Geoff thought, and he was suddenly caught again by that strange sense of contentment. A feeling of satisfaction that came from somewhere deep inside, and that made him want to smile, for no real reason at all.

He looked around the room. Most of the furniture had come from Mrs Murphy, and it was good to know the old lady was a lot happier these days. She had decided not to take any more pills, and found she was no longer seeing or hearing things. She and Mrs Baxter had taken to going to the cinema together a couple of afternoons a week, and on Friday evenings the boys did her weekly shopping at Tesco's. It was in return for this that she had offered them anything they wanted from the odd bits of old furniture she had stored in her garage and attic.

They had taken an elderly sofa, a carpet, a kitchen table and chairs, a table lamp, a black and white television, and the radiogram. There was no electricity in the tower, of course, but Aquila could power anything electrical up to a range of two hundred metres. It could also blanket any sound or light in the room, so that nobody outside could hear or see what was going on. Aquila could do so many things. Tom had once asked it to list them all, but abandoned the idea when it turned out the list would take three and half days to read.

On the wall along from the table was a set of shelves holding the rocks and fossils that Tom had collected over the last few weeks. There were bits of coloured sandstone from the Isle of Wight, chunks of hexagonal basalt from Staffa in Scotland, and on the bottom shelf, pride of the collection, the pointed piece of granite that had once been the top of the Matterhorn. Aquila's laser had sliced it off like a knob of butter and one day, thought Geoff, someone was going to notice that the highest mountain in the Alps was only 4,477.2 metres high instead of 4,477.5.

The wall above the sofa was where Geoff kept his trophies. There was the photo of him standing beside the statue at the top of Nelson's column. There was the hat that he had snatched from President Clinton on his state visit to London. There were the bails from the last Test match played against Pakistan, and a couple of fading chrysanthemums that he had picked from the gardens at Buckingham Palace.

'All finished.' Tom put down his pen, and stood up. Normally he liked to check his homework with Aquila, but he could do that later. He came over and stood by his friend. 'How was the lesson?'

Geoff shrugged. 'It was OK.'

Geoff would never admit it but, in fact, his lessons with Miss Stevenson were a lot more than OK. She worked with an efficiency that had won his respect, and a sense of humour he had come to appreciate.

Above all, she was a woman who knew how to do her job, and for the first time in his life Geoff had begun to find the world of words and letters beginning to make some sort of sense. It had been a revelation. He had started reading road signs, odd words from the television, and the belief was beginning to grow that one day he would –

'This trip this afternoon.' Tom interrupted his thoughts. 'I've got everything packed, but . . . would you mind if we did America tomorrow?'

'Tomorrow?'

'It's Mum,' Tom explained. 'She's arranged to visit these cousins in Stockport, and she wants me to go with her.'

Mrs Baxter had been arranging a good many trips since she had taken delivery of her car. Most days she visited some branch of the family or an old friend, and all this on top of the cinema trips with Mrs Murphy and the evening classes in Japanese swordsmanship. It was as if she was trying to make up for three years of staying at home by doing three times as much as everyone else.

Tom looked at his watch. 'I think we'd have to allow at least two hours for New York to be on the safe side, and I said I'd be home by half one. Of course, if you want to go on your own . . .'

'No, no, tomorrow'll be fine.' Still holding his mug of chocolate, Geoff climbed into Aquila. 'We'll just go somewhere else. Somewhere closer.'

Again, he felt that curious upsurge of happiness.

It bubbled up in his mind but, annoyingly, he still couldn't put his finger on where it came from.

Tom picked up the bag with the packed lunches and swung himself into Aquila beside Geoff. Neither of them bothered with coats these days. Wherever they flew, Aquila could keep the temperature at any level you asked.

'I'll take her up, shall I?' he said. 'Till you've finished your drink.'

As Tom took the controls, Aquila floated gently out of the tower into the sunshine. From beneath them came the buzz of traffic from the town, the sound of the breeze ruffling through the trees, and the noise of children playing over in the park.

'Where do you want to go then?'

For a moment, Geoff did not reply. He suddenly had the feeling that he had turned an important corner. It was as if he had been climbing a particularly perilous, steep stretch in an upward path, and now found himself on broad open ground again with the road stretching invitingly ahead. He felt he had understood something for the first time, only he couldn't quite think what it was.

'It's your turn to choose, isn't it?'

Tom waited patiently, but Geoff still did not reply. He was concentrating hard. If he concentrated, he knew he would find the answer that floated tantalizingly out of reach, somewhere in the top of his mind . . .

'There's lots of things we could do.' Tom stared

up at the sky. 'We could fly over to the National Park if you wanted. See this axe thing Doctor Warner's so excited about . . .'

He nearly had it, Geoff thought. It was almost in his grasp . . .

'Or we could go to Paris again,' Tom continued. 'Find out if your chewing gum's still stuck on the top of the Eiffel Tower.' He paused. 'We can do anything really.'

'That's it!' A slow smile spread across Geoff's face. 'That's it, isn't it?'

'What?'

'That's the whole point! We can go wherever we want!'

'Yes . . .' said Tom. Frankly it seemed a bit obvious, but he decided not to say anything. For some reason, Geoff seemed to think it was important.

'You find yourself an eagle, and you can go where you like. Anywhere.' Geoff seemed entranced by the concept. 'Anywhere at all . . .'

'Right.' Tom nodded. There was a long pause, until Tom eventually asked, 'So . . . where do you want to go then?'

'I'm not sure.' Geoff sipped his mug of chocolate. 'But I think, first, I'd like to go . . . up.'

'Up?'

'Up high.' Geoff nodded. 'I want to see the view.'

Tom shrugged. 'OK.'

Aquila started to rise. Higher and higher, gathering speed as it went, until the noises faded, and first the people and then the cars and even the buildings ceased to be separate entities, and all of Stavely became just an irregular circle in the surrounding green of the countryside and the noise faded to a deep silence.

And still they climbed. Up and up, soaring into the sky until, even if Aquila had not been invisible, from the ground it would have been too small to see. It was a perfect day, and Tom could see wisps of cloud floating far below casting tiny shadows on the ground beneath.

'Is this high enough?' he asked.

'I would say . . .' Geoff turned and smiled at his friend. 'I would say that we've hardly started.'

It all started with a Scarecrow

Puffin is well over sixty years old.
Sounds ancient, doesn't it? But Puffin has never been
so lively. We're always on the lookout for the next big
idea, which is how it began all those years ago.

Penguin Books was a big idea from the mind of
a man called Allen Lane, who in 1935 invented
the quality paperback and changed the world.
**And from great Penguins, great Puffins grew,
changing the face of children's books forever.**

The first four Puffin Picture Books were hatched in 1940 and the
first Puffin story book featured a man with broomstick arms called
Worzel Gummidge. In 1967 Kaye Webb, Puffin Editor, started the
Puffin Club, promising to **'make children into readers'.**
She kept that promise and over 200,000 children became
devoted Puffineers through their quarterly instalments of
Puffin Post, which is now back for a new generation.

Many years from now, we hope you'll look back and
remember Puffin with a smile. **No matter what your age
or what you're into, there's a Puffin for everyone.**
The possibilities are endless, but one thing is for sure:
whether it's a picture book or a paperback, a sticker book
or a hardback, **if it's got that little Puffin
on it – it's bound to be good.**